GAITO

THE BEGGAR
AND OTHER STORIES

Translated from the Russian
and with an Introduction
by Bryan Karetnyk

PUSHKIN PRESS
LONDON

Pushkin Press
71–75 Shelton Street
London, WC2H 9JQ

Despite all efforts, the publisher has been unable to ascertain the owner of the rights to the original Russian text. We welcome any further information on the matter.

English translation and introduction © Bryan Karetnyk 2018

'Maître Rueil' was first published in *Chisla* in Paris, 1931
'Happiness' was first published in *Sovremennye zapiski* in Paris, 1932
'Deliverance' was first published in *Sovremennye zapiski* in Paris, 1936
'The Mistake' was first published in *Sovremennye zapiski* in Paris, 1938
'The Beggar' was first published in *Mosty* in Munich, 1962
'Ivanov's Letters' was first published in *Novyi zhurnal* in New York, 1963

First published by Pushkin Press in 2018

Published with the support of the Institute for Literary Translation (Russia)

AD VERBUM

1 3 5 7 9 8 6 4 2

ISBN 13: 978-1-78227-401-8

All rights reserved. No part of this publication may be reproduced, stored in a retrieval system or transmitted in any form or by any means, electronic, mechanical, photocopying, recording or otherwise, without prior permission in writing from Pushkin Press

Frontispiece: Gaito Gazdanov in the 1920s, Paris

Designed and typeset by Tetragon, London

Proudly printed and bound in Great Britain by
TJ International, Padstow, Cornwall

www.pushkinpress.com

CONTENTS

Introduction 7

THE BEGGAR AND OTHER STORIES

Maître Rueil	19
Happiness	47
Deliverance	101
The Mistake	135
The Beggar	159
Ivanov's Letters	187

INTRODUCTION

In a letter of 1960 to the author and critic Leonid Rzhevsky, Gaito Gazdanov, then approaching the last decade of his life and career, wrote with characteristic self-effacement: "It wouldn't be difficult for me to put together a book of [my own] short stories, but I'm still not convinced that it's necessary." Time and again Gazdanov demurred, and never did oversee a collection of his stories. In fact, only once, at the very start of his career, had he ever seriously considered editing a selection of his short fiction at all, as part of an envisaged—though never realized—eight-volume collected works. While this prospective tome, tentatively titled *Hawaiian Guitars* (after an early story first published in 1930), would have included Gazdanov's juvenilia, the absence of any precedent set by the mature author looking back over his long career creates both an opportunity and a dilemma for an editor: what to include in this first English collection of his short fiction?

Over the course of five decades, Gazdanov wrote a total of nine complete novels (and a further two that were never finished) as well as over fifty short stories, all of which were published individually in the many émigré journals, reviews and newspapers scattered across Europe and North America. The collapse of the Soviet Union twenty years after Gazdanov's death enabled a "grand return" to his homeland, where each of his works without exception has since been republished, many of them enjoying regular reprinting. So, too, in France—Gazdanov's adoptive homeland—his works have received considerable attention over the last quarter-century, with several volumes of his short stories appearing in translation in recent years. For English audiences, however, the picture is rather different. While just over half of Gazdanov's novels are now available in English translation, his short stories have been greatly overlooked. With that in mind, it seemed paramount to privilege here those of Gazdanov's stories that have never before appeared in English, as well as those which together represent the best of his work. The stories that follow have been drawn from his two most prolific and successful periods of short-prose writing: first the 1930s, as a young writer basking in the spectacular success of his debut novel, *An Evening with Claire*; and latterly the 1960s, as a mature author in the ripeness of age and creative practice, at the acme of his artistic talent.

Although the earliest story in this collection dates to 1931, Gazdanov's first story in fact appeared as early as

1926, when he was a mere twenty-two. Having arrived in Paris as a refugee some three years earlier, and with memories of the Revolution and Civil War fresh in his mind, he had spent the winter of 1925–26 sleeping rough in the city's streets and the underpasses of the Métro. At the time of that first story's publication he was working as a driller at the Citroën factory in Javel. The following year a stroke of luck brought him a job with the major French publishing house Hachette; however, contrary to what one might expect of an aspiring author, he soon quit, oppressed by the bureaucracy and tedium of the industry, and took up work as a night-taxi driver. This unconventional employment, which for almost a quarter of a century constituted a dependable provision against the vagaries of publishing, would be the career for which (aside from writing) Gazdanov would always be remembered, lending him the lifelong moniker "*l'écrivain-chauffeur*".

The stories Gazdanov wrote during these tumultuous first years of exile came out in Prague, and constituted his first step towards serious recognition. Set predominantly in revolutionary Russia, they combine settings, characters and a narrative style reminiscent of Isaac Babel's short-story cycles with a fashionable degree of typographical experimentation. Yet in a time when language and literature were conspicuously politicized, this "kaleidoscopic" style, which imparted a fragmentariness and episodic quality aimed at conveying the "crisis of the age", proved an unpopular choice among the more conservative doyens of émigré belles-lettres, who openly— and vociferously—shunned such outré experimentation, associating it with the much-maligned Soviet avant-garde. Seeing in themselves the true heirs and torch-bearers of the Russian national school, they believed it the emigration's sacred duty to ensure that literature follow the path laid out by the classics, unbroken by the rupture of 1917. Yet Gazdanov was never one to follow suit. As his art matured, it continued to break conventions, and his artist's voice would prove one of the most individual and distinctive of his generation.

Gazdanov's golden age of short-story writing dawned in the years immediately after his novelistic debut with *An Evening with Claire*, which came out in December 1929 and soon won accolades in all corners of the émigré literary beau monde. In the wake of this success, he began publishing his work in ever more prestigious venues, including a radical new journal, *Chisla* ("Numbers"). Founded in reaction to the conservatism of the influential "thick journals", it aimed at giving a voice to the younger generation of poets and prose writers in exile. Here, in the journal's fifth issue, flanked by and interspersed with reproductions of paintings by Mikhail Larionov and Natalia Goncharova, originally appeared the first story of this collection, 'Maître Rueil' (1931). Though by now having discarded his avant-garde aesthetic in favour of a more classical elegance, Gazdanov retains the motley cast of eccentric international characters and thrillerish plot that are the hallmark of his earlier works. Playing provocatively on one of the émigré's most conspicuous fears (espionage as well as the kidnapping and even murder of high-profile figures by the Soviet secret police were not without basis in reality), Gazdanov transfigures the popular genre with an underlying philosophical tract, metaphorizing the "sad meaninglessness" of life's journey in the protagonist's mission to Soviet Moscow. The haunting sense of melancholy and dislocation permeating the work also imparts yet a further layer of existential tension to the story, while the striking series of hallucinatory scenes that blur the boundaries between dream and reality foreshadows Gazdanov's later metaphysical thrillers.

How ironic it was that Gazdanov's success in the radical *Chisla* should only pave the way for his entry into the established canon of émigré greats. That same year, in 1931, he debuted in that most prestigious of thick journals, *Sovremennye zapiski* ("Contemporary annals"), and it was there that he placed the next three stories included in this collection. These works of the mid–late 1930s engage in an ever-weightier dialogue with the classical canon in their narrative style and thematic exposition, while transforming recognizable plots through the introduction of exilic settings and an engagement with European literatures and philosophies. Gazdanov's protagonists are a series of unfortunate individuals, each struggling with humanity's eternal questions, which for many émigrés had been cast into sharp relief by the wilderness of exile. Experiencing profound loss, the Job-like protagonist of 'Happiness' (1932) is forced to contend with the nature and possibilities of life amid suffering and tragic misfortune. 'Deliverance' (1936), a secular variation on Tolstoy's *The Death of Ivan Ilyich*, is a philosophical meditation on the primacy and arbitrariness of death. It probes the paradox that while all desires and actions lead inexorably towards destruction, and while in the face of death all things are ultimately futile, a life devoid of beauty and sensual pleasure is nevertheless one of "unbearable horror".

'The Mistake' (1938) continues Gazdanov's excavation of the canon. The story, originally titled 'Betrayal', served as a preliminary sketch for his most Tolstoyan of novels, *The Flight*, which, with its complex web of family relationships and adultery, is an overt refashioning of *Anna Karenina* in the tradition of Chekhov's 'Anna on the

INTRODUCTION

Neck'. 'The Mistake' presents us with a psychological drama in miniature, a devastating portrayal of a woman's infidelity and the acute repercussions it has for her and her family. Dissolving the nineteenth-century horror of female sexuality, Gazdanov's narrative leads inescapably towards an astonishing denouement that probes the orthodoxies of morality.

This modernist "making new" of the classics proved contentious still. Despite Gazdanov's widely acclaimed stylistic virtuosity, there followed accusations of literary *inostranshchina*, or "Esperantism", a pernicious brand of exoticism that supposedly arose from the influence of foreign literatures and threatened the precarious, nostalgic streak of nationalism running through Russian exilic literature. Yet the voguishness of the criticism notwithstanding, Gazdanov in fact found himself in excellent company: two of the emigration's foremost critics—"the two Georges", Adamovich and Ivanov—had been levelling those same accusations against Gazdanov's greatest rival, Vladimir Nabokov, for years.

As the decade drew on, short prose gave way to larger works. The years immediately before, during and after the war represent the single most intensive period of novel-writing in Gazdanov's career. The first three instalments of *The Flight*, his third novel, were published serially in

1939, before the war put paid to the publication of the novel's fourth and final part. His subsequent novel, *Night Road*, was luckier, coming out in full in the final two issues of *Sovremennye zapiski*, just before the journal was forcibly liquidated after the Nazi occupation of Paris in 1940. Nevertheless, while the war in Europe may have halted the publication of Gazdanov's work, it did not stop him writing—though his mode and reading public did alter temporarily. From 1942 to 1945 Gazdanov and his wife, the Greek Odessan Faina Lamzaki, worked for the Resistance in Paris, helping Soviet partisans and editing an underground information bulletin.

Gazdanov's hiatus in short prose writing after the war came about for a variety of reasons. For one, the wartime demise of many European journals meant that writers now had to look increasingly further afield for venues in which to place their new writing. Gazdanov found a publisher for almost all his post-war fiction on the other side of the Atlantic in Mikhail Zetlin and Mark Aldanov's New York-based *Novyi zhurnal* ("The new review"), which not only published the vast majority of his stories, but also serialized his last five novels, including the much-fêted *The Spectre of Alexander Wolf* and *The Buddha's Return*. The scarcity of journals, however, was not the only impediment to Gazdanov's return to short fiction. Having turned down the offer of an editorship at the Chekhov Publishing House in New York in 1952, he opted to take up a job in Munich on Radio Liberty's Russia desk the following year. The intense demands of radio journalism triggered a sharp drop in his literary output, meaning that he would publish hardly any creative writing again until the end of the decade. Happily enough, the decline was only temporary, and the resurgence of creative activity towards 1960 ushered in a splendid new period in the author's career.

Gazdanov's last decade saw the publication of some of his finest stories: 'Requiem' (1960), 'The Beggar' (1962) and 'Ivanov's Letters' (1963), each a masterpiece in its own right. These late works present crystalline distillations of the aesthetics and philosophies that Gazdanov had explored more extensively in his long fiction: the cruces of happiness and fate, the sovereignty of the metaphysical, the richness of the inner life in counterpoint with physical poverty, and the metamorphoses of the soul throughout life's journey into death. They simultaneously cast a retrospective look over his *œuvre* at large, much in the same way as does his final novel, *Evelyn and Her Friends*. In this decade, Gazdanov's preoccupation with the mystery of death reached its apogee: these inspired last works constitute his ultimate, elegiac exploration of life's transmutation into art and, at the same time, a reflection on the very *raison d'être* of art, and of life itself.

While Gazdanov may have harboured doubts about the need for a volume of his short stories, I believe it is safe to say that the necessity of such a collection in English is indisputable. Which works he might have chosen himself will for ever remain a mystery; however, in selecting and translating the six stories that follow, I hope I have done the author and his work some justice—and in this endeavour perhaps, just this once, proved the *maître*, "the master", wrong.

B.S.K.

THE BEGGAR
AND OTHER STORIES

MAÎTRE RUEIL

(1931)

M<small>AÎTRE RUEIL</small>, a Frenchman, blond with black eyes and a sharp, square face, an agent of the Sûreté Générale, had been dispatched from Paris to Moscow on an important political assignment. In the days in which this story takes place he was around thirty years old; he had long since graduated from the Faculty of Law at the University of Paris and for eight years or so had been engaged exclusively in political affairs, which brought in a sizeable income and allowed him, who had no fortune of his own, to live in great style. He enjoyed a reputation as one of France's finest agents; and the word *maître*, by which he was known and to which, by virtue of his legal learning, he had the right, rather frequently acquired another, more deferential, character: Maître Rueil was truly head and shoulders above all his colleagues. A brilliant career lay ahead of him. In addition to the purely professional dexterity, essential in people of his occupation, he was endowed with many other gifts. He spoke several languages fluently, could catch the meaning of others from only half a word, never lost his nerve on dangerous assignments, and was rewarded with exceptional success in everything he laid his hands on. It was said that the shadow of good fortune followed him everywhere.

He was of below-average height but very strong; years of continuous physical training and intense mental exertion had made of him an almost infallible human mechanism. The maître's nervous system was in perfect working order: even the frequent sleepless nights had no ill effect on him. He endured journeys of any length with ease, was able to sleep in any location, was never burdened by the tedium of endless trips and never knew what it meant to be seasick. Because he was young and in rude health—and also, very likely, because of his constant efforts of imagination, directed at the solution of dangerous, though purely practical, problems—abstract ideas never drew his interest. His penetration extended well beyond his charge of duties—into the realms of ethics, philosophy and art—and was so great as to allow him, should the occasion present itself, to construct and defend all manner of systems of ideas; such an occasion, however, had yet to present itself—and so the maître's knowledge lay there, dormant and inert. Maître Rueil could not admit the thought that, if it were set in motion, it would spell catastrophe for him: in the mental landscape surrounding Maître Rueil, nothing was supposed to happen that could not be foreseen to a greater or lesser degree of approximation.

Then, one day, when boarding a ship from Marseilles to Constantinople, the maître suddenly experienced a sensation hitherto unknown to him, one of incomprehensible irritation and utterly inexplicable alarm. No one was there to see him off: he had no family and had deemed it unnecessary to divulge his plans to anyone. Only one figure, in a hat and a tattered blazer, with a face on which there was a decorative blue mole below the left eye, appeared on the quayside at the last moment and immediately vanished, having met the maître's gaze. This was the man whom the stubborn, stupid officials of the Sûreté Générale's lower ranks invariably dispatched to ascertain whether the maître was indeed departing. Once, after returning from a routine trip, the maître went to see the bureau chief, who was in charge of agents, and, laughing especially calmly and coldly, told him that he thought he was a fool. The bureau chief remained silent, for he greatly feared that Maître Rueil, using his influence, could have him fired. However, the maître did nothing of the sort—and the bureau chief, each time fearing more than on the previous occasion, would again send the man to follow the maître, because he considered it his professional duty.

It was cold and beginning to get dark. Scraps of paper, broken boards and glittering oily slicks danced upon the filthy waves. The ship had long been standing on the roads, and Maître Rueil gazed absent-mindedly ahead and saw the nearby quay lighting up and black boats moored to the bank. Then he took several turns about the deck and, after waiting for the first movements of the propeller, whipping up foam instantaneously, went below.

There were few passengers: a Catholic priest, a tall, slight man of around forty-five and a great lover of anecdotes; a young Greek with quick movements and thievish eyes; and a hulking boxer, a thickset titan from Buenos Aires. The boxer was unable to lay to rest his recent defeat and was for the fourth time telling of how the referee had been far from impartial. He was speaking in English; the priest listened to him with manifest pleasure, yet at times he would laugh at inappropriate moments and again fall silent under the boxer's heavy gaze. Taking the maître by the arm, he said:

"Just imagine, I'm not in the least bored by this story. I don't speak English. Praise be!"

Maître Rueil politely smiled, with his lips alone.

Apart from the priest, the Greek and the boxer, there was a tall lady in a blue dress travelling on board the ship—an actress from Odessa, with a proud, troubled face; on her heels followed a short-legged Russian, a businessman to all appearances: the tense expression on his face attested to his unremitting readiness to execute her every wish at the drop of a hat. Maître Rueil watched the actress and felt a sense of envy towards the Russian. "*Très bien, la petite?*"*—there suddenly came a voice from behind him. The maître turned around and saw the priest's grinning face.

Maître Rueil sat down in an armchair, lit his pipe and made an effort to forget the alarming, piercing feeling that had so recently set in, and which might be likened to the foreboding of some misfortune, were this not the first time in all his life that such a feeling had befallen the maître. However, despite a certain abstraction, the maître, as was his wont, still managed to mark those little details that seemed most distinctive upon a superficial examination of the passengers: the Russian's fat wallet (the businessman had moved it from one pocket to another while rummaging for some newspaper clipping), the Greek's roving eyes, the complex web of red veins on the priest's face and the

---

* "Nice little thing, isn't she?"

darned elbows of the boxer's jacket. "He's short on cash," thought the maître. "Then again, it's possible that this is his travelling suit and that he's just thrifty." "Unlikely," the maître answered himself, and here for the first time noticed that the ship was beginning to pitch. "Unlikely: he isn't shrewd enough for that."

By now the lights of Marseilles had disappeared. The maître was sitting with his eyes half shut; his head was slightly buzzing, although he had had nothing to drink. He was no longer observing his fellow passengers, although a little earlier his attention had been attracted by the actress and the boxer: the boxer because he was a marvellous specimen of the athletic form, and the actress because a recollection of her forced the maître to stretch for a moment and to move and tense the muscles in his body. And suddenly it seemed to the maître as if he had sailed on board this ship and seen these people all before, as if long, long ago he had sailed the sea just like this and felt that same strange ennui, and that afterwards for a long while he had languished half-conscious in the dark, and when he had opened his eyes again, he had already forgotten everything. The ship pitched more and more violently. The actress instantly began to feel seasick; for some reason or other, with a frightened look, her companion dashed into their cabin. The actress's body convulsed; the skin on her face turned ashen. The maître drew his eyes away from her and saw the boxer, whose enormous figure was bent double: he was groaning and shaking his head. The priest's gaze, directed heavenward, seemed surprisingly nonsensical to the maître. The young Greek, who was not suffering from the pitching, slapped the priest on the back; the latter turned around to point out to the Greek the impropriety of his behaviour, but he only looked at him and sighed, and was unable to utter a single word.

Maître Rueil retired to his cabin. It was almost eleven o'clock in the evening. The maître detected in his throat the unpalatable aftertaste of the macaroni that had been served at dinner; the thrifty cook must have prepared it using rancid butter. The maître lay on his berth and closed his eyes, thinking that any minute now he would fall asleep, as usual. But sleep escaped him. The pitching grew ever more exaggerated: his cabin slid away and then righted itself—now from right to left, now up and down. Diving and surfacing thus on his berth, Maître Rueil followed the erratic shadows on the floor, which followed in time with the motion of the shuddering and revolving lamp. The macaroni's unpleasant taste intensified, as did the slight ringing in his ears and head. "I'm ill," thought Maître Rueil for the first time. The door to his cabin seemed to be slowly opening. He looked more carefully; the door was still. But sitting in the maître's chair was the boxer, who—it was unclear when or how—had entered his cabin. "What do you want?" asked the maître. But the boxer made no reply; and so the maître decided to leave him in peace. "Just how did he get in here?" wondered the maître, then instantly forgot about the question. The ship continued to pitch. Maître Rueil watched the boxer and with each roll of the cabin seemed to draw closer to him; yet the armchair invariably imitated the motion of the cabin and remained forever out of reach. The sea's heavy tumult merged with the ringing in his ears, and when Maître Rueil tried speaking aloud he was unable to hear his own voice. The maître fell silent; he remained in this unfamiliar world of images and sounds; their alarming immateriality never ceased its torment.

"The boxer," thought the maître with an effort, and his berth slowly floated towards the armchair. "The boxer travels and makes his money with his fists. Then he'll return to his Buenos Aires and learn something nasty: for instance, that his wife has a lover. It's bound to be unpleasant."

The ship was being tossed from side to side. The maître, eyes fixed on the boxer, went on thinking:

"Yes, but then those wonderful muscles will become soft, and no woman…" He couldn't remember what "no woman" would do. "Yes, no woman will want to belong to him… Unless, of course, he pays for it. But then he won't have any need of women. And all that will be left are death and memories."

Strange and unexpected, Maître Rueil recalled a young Italian. It was when the maître was living in Milan and thanks to his efforts the Italian police uncovered an anarchist plot. The youth the maître recalled was one of the party activists and Rueil's closest comrade. During the interrogation, having found out that the maître was a Frenchman and a provocateur, he shouted in his face:

"*On te rappelera ça un jour!*"*

"*Vous êtes un comédien*,"† the maître had replied.

"Now he's in prison," thought the maître. "Of course, the actor was me, not him. What will happen when he's released and bumps into me?… I'm not afraid of him. But what will I say to him? I'm ill," said the maître, coming to his senses.

The agitation eased at once. The maître's former clarity of thought returned to him for a time. "It's all stuff and nonsense," he said. "It's just a rare variety of seasickness." Yet still sleep eluded him, and for a long while he tossed and turned on his berth. An old nursery rhyme

---

* "You'll live to regret this."
† Literally, "You're a play-actor"; figuratively here, "That's a good one."

suddenly floated into his thoughts, and he immediately recalled even its simple melody:

> *Quand j'étais petit*
> *Je n'étais pas grand,*
> *J'allais à l'école*
> *Comme les petits enfants.**

The maître smiled with the satisfaction of having remembered the melody and began quietly to sing, and, as he did, he thought that this children's tune was the best thing there had been in his life. "All the rest," he told himself with a smile, "was business, money, women and restaurants—all that was sordid and superfluous. But this is good:

> *Quand j'étais petit*
> *Je n'étais pas grand…*"

He glanced at the chair and saw that the boxer was gone. So much the better. Immediately there came a knock; the door opened and in came the Russian actress: she wore a light dressing gown and slippers. However, Maître Rueil, smiling, looked at her, saw her barely covered, simmering

---

* When I was little / I wasn't big, / I went to school / Like the little kids.

body—and just lay there. "*Monsieur*," said the actress, and the maître smiled politely and wistfully, almost not hearing her. "*Monsieur*," she repeated deliriously, "*voulez-vous tromper mon amant avec moi?*"*

The maître wanted to laugh. "Could she really comprehend," he thought with a jolly expression on his face, "that all this is entirely superfluous and inconsequential?"

"*Non, madame,*" he said, barely able to contain his laughter. "*Non, madame, je n'en ai aucune envie.*"†

Thereupon the actress left at once, slamming the door—and Maître Rueil stopped laughing. "What did I do?" he said; and all the terrible senselessness of his action became clear to him. "Did I refuse her? Two days ago I would have paid serious money for that. I'm ill!" he shouted. "I'm ill! I'm ill!"

He fidgeted around on the berth; an almighty headache was impeding his thought. He stretched out and, at last, fell asleep.

The ship was on the approach to Constantinople. Over the bright waters of the Bosphorus flew innumerable white specks of seagulls, resembling from afar fleecy, moving clouds that scattered on contact with the sea and then

---

* "Would you like to cuckold my lover, sir?"
† "No, madam, I have no such desire."

soared up again, hovering in the limpid air. All the passengers had come out on deck, and the Greek, standing beside the boxer, explained to him:

"There is Pera, over there Galata, and there Stamboul."

They sailed along the coast; white and yellow villas rose up from the water, the peaks of minarets glittered: the sun was shining brightly, and it was warm. From the quayside there came a shrill, unbroken clamour; heavy little boats with rowing Turks, standing with their backs aft-facing and plunging the oars deep into the water, crossed the Bosphorus in all directions. At the bridge connecting Stamboul with the European part of the city there thronged a multitude of people, and the maître recalled that when he had arrived into Constantinople for the first time and seen this great assemblage of humanity in one place, he had thought there must have been some catastrophe. The ship meanwhile went slower and slower and, finally, came to a halt on the roads; rowing boats immediately swarmed around it. Ferrymen, interrupting one another, offered their boats, and the maître heard a high-pitched but clearly masculine voice, shouting in Russian:

"No, I won't go! He'll drown us!"

The boat, however, was already getting under way, and the Turk was rowing with contemptuous composure, paying no heed whatever to the cries of his passenger; in the bay there was a considerably strong swell. The Catholic priest spent a long time haggling, but at last he too reached an agreement and got into a boat, absorbed in his red missal.

Maître Rueil hired a ferryman without haggling. The Turk, astonished by his generosity, rowed with great zeal and, after a short while, overtook both of the other boats that had set off earlier. The maître bowed to the actress, who in reply shrugged her shoulders scornfully. Then her companion stood up and beamed at the maître, but immediately fell, having lost his foothold.

The two days that Maître Rueil spent in Constantinople were passed in that same unaccountable sense of anguish and alarm. At night he slept terribly, having the most unusual dreams: rivers covered by ice, exceedingly like crêpe paper, an abbot who was for some reason riding a bicycle, and an anarchist youth who sidled up to him and said:

*"Il y a quelque chose qui ne marche pas, mon cher maître?"**

The maître awoke, smoked half a pipe and fell asleep again. Towards morning he awoke for the fourth or fifth

---

* "Is something the matter, my dear maître?"

time. "I must go for a walk outside, I need some fresh air," he thought hazily. He dressed and left the hotel. It was very early; weedy little old men were carrying heavy crates with oil and vegetables; Turks selling *bublik*s were trudging around in the morning mist. Somewhere nearby an invisible donkey was braying. The maître walked through Pera, heading towards the Galata steps; a couple of drowsy sailors caught his eye. Suddenly he saw something very odd: the tall building he was walking past began slowly and silently to tilt; the figure of the Russian actress appeared on the second floor and floated down, gripping the window frame. The maître paused—and caught the boxer's hoarse voice, which said in a tone of friendly caution:

"You ought to be more careful, dear maître, such journeys might lead you to no good."

The maître turned around. That moment a sharp crack rang out; a woman's soft arms enfolded the maître, and the building's dark wall suddenly came to rest above his head.

Later it gradually began to grow light, objects became more discernible, and Maître Rueil assured himself that he was in bed in his hotel room. Over coffee, while talking with his neighbour, who was reading *Le Matin* and bitterly upbraiding the French judicial system, which enabled the repeated acquittal of "green-eyed, gun-toting women", as he put it, the maître forgot all about his dream. He learnt that the first ship bound for Sebastopol was to set sail only the following morning—that is why that evening, after dark, he resolved to set out on a stroll about the city, declining the services of the guide they would try to foist upon him.

He sauntered through Pera, saw that nothing new had appeared there, and decided to head for the part of town he didn't know. He selected at random one of the narrow little side streets running to the right of Pera, and walked down it at length, cut across the large Turkish cemetery with the crooked marble pillars of its monuments, and wound up in Kasımpaşa. He went farther and farther on, turning several times and never worrying about where the road would lead him—and when the desire to return finally did seize him, he meandered in vain for half an hour and found his way back to a place where he had already been and to which he had no intention of returning. For some time he wandered the empty narrow streets, between wooden houses with grilles over the windows, and realized that without the help of someone he would find it difficult getting out of this labyrinth. There was darkness all around: a pitiful kerosene lamp was all there was to illuminate the dry stones of the uneven pavement and the layer of grey dust coating the steps of the nearest house. The maître stood there for about ten minutes. There was no one to be seen. Then a tall, angular Turk in a turban walked past, but he made no reply when the maître asked whether he could show him the way to Pera. When the maître, bristling now, tried to approach the Turk, the latter suddenly broke into a run. Aware of the absurdity of a pursuit, the maître nevertheless ran after him and, of course, would have caught up with him; however, the Turk dived into some back alley, and the maître was left standing in the street. Shrugging his shoulders and cursing every Turk on the earth, the maître steeled himself to walk briskly and tried just not to err from the direction he had decided on. Half an hour later he was in Galata, in a little restaurant; the Greek proprietor was arguing heatedly with some exotic sailor attired in a hussar's jacket; in the corner a blind old man was playing a pandura while his young guide sat quietly beside him, his sunburnt legs, bare below the knees and covered in golden down, placed under him. A dark-haired girl in a vermilion jacket and a grey chequered skirt took a seat next to the maître and said to him in English, almost incidentally: "I love you, darling."

The maître looked at her and said nothing.

"I love you, my dear compatriot," she said in Russian.

The maître again said nothing. But the girl was not at all put off by this. She placed her hands to her heart, cracked her fingers and said, with perfect French pronunciation:

"*Je vous aime, mon chéri.*"

"*J'aurai voulu vous répondre de la meme façon,*"* said the maître sharply at last. But the girl didn't understand his response, for she knew only one phrase in French. She began to curse, mixing Turkish, Hebrew and Greek words, and the maître gave her a lira so that she would be quiet. For this he received a sticky kiss; she embraced him, his eyes darkened, and he recalled his latest dream. "Why is it that I only chance upon what I already know?" he muttered, getting to his feet; the Greek proprietor, smiling and setting in motion all the flesh on his face, saw him to the door. The maître walked to his hotel without paying attention to anything and without seeing the lights on the Bosphorus, the curling grapevines on the ancient walls, the nearby white buildings of Nişantaşı looming amid the dusky air, or the squat little stone eagles on the German consulate building.

A day later the maître was in Sebastopol.

---

* "Would that I could answer you in the same way."

He was sitting on a bench in the Primorsky Boulevard, smoking. Beside him sat Smirnov, one of the Sûreté Générale's Russian agents, well known in those circles, a very energetic and lively fellow—and an old classmate of the maître's from the Sorbonne, to boot. Smirnov was telling the maître, peppering his rapid speech all the while with complex tenses—"*Il avait fallu que je lui donnasse quelque chose*"*—what he thought ought to be done.

"I'm very glad they assigned this to you: Fortune favours you. Without luck you couldn't do a thing there; you wouldn't manage to sniff out this scoundrel even with hounds. They offered the case to me, but I refused: I'd be recognized there immediately, even if I wore Turkish trousers and a chokha. But I must warn you that you're dealing with serious people here."

He paused.

"*Ils n'ont pas froid aux yeux*,"† he said, continuing to think of those people whom the maître would encounter. "But truly, only in danger is there pleasure and allure."

The maître didn't reply at once. "Don't you think?" asked Smirnov.

Before their eyes stood several trees; beyond the trees they glimpsed the smooth, glittering sea. In the distance

---

* "I had to give him something."
† "They fear nothing."

the outline of the Mikhailovsky Fortress rose out of the deep-blue water; to the right the leaden mountains towered up. Somehow it felt very empty; a wind was blowing, bells were ringing in the town; the sparkling of the sea, the sombre gleam of the lilac clay on the bank, the lugubrious peal of the bell and the still, bright air inexplicably—but unmistakably for the maître—accentuated his terrible impotence and loneliness. The ennui that had seized only one part of his consciousness at the journey's outset had now taken possession of him irrevocably.

"What? Yes, of course," he said distractedly. "Only it's all meaningless and futile."

"What is meaningless?" asked Smirnov, not comprehending. Maître Rueil was astonished that Smirnov had failed to grasp such a simple and self-evident observation, that political affairs and the allure of danger were but trivial, foolish things. However, he wanted neither to argue nor to share his feelings with Smirnov.

"Yes, you're right, naturally," he said. "I only meant that there's no point wasting time waiting." With an effort the maître produced this unconvincing explanation.

"The waiting always comes to an end," replied Smirnov. "But I haven't yet told you all that I must." And so at length Smirnov told the maître of the people whose acquaintance might be of some use to him. Those were:

Monsieur Jean, a Russian *rentier*,* as Smirnov described him; Madame Rose, the owner of a private institution in Moscow, a very dear lady and, what's more, a Parisian; and the student Corot: he was a strongman so this was only in the case of a ruckus. "And, of course, the main man, on meeting whom hangs the success of your mission." He described a young man of twenty-three, a *bon vivant* and a gambler, a cunning, wary and dangerous adversary. The maître to all appearances seemed to be following Smirnov's rapid French patter, but in fact he was scarcely listening to him. He was thinking of entirely inconsequential things: whether Smirnov was married, whether he had old flames, whether indeed he had loved anyone. These thoughts, so unusual for the maître, surprised even him. "Who is Smirnov?" he asked himself. "A man who has done various things all his life and, essentially, never known why he has done them—perhaps he doesn't need to know. What was it all for? Anyway, it's all nonsense in the final reckoning."

Concluding the conversation, Smirnov got to his feet first. "Well, all the best," he said to the maître. "*Bonne chance*."† And with that he left. The maître remained seated; he lit his pipe, threw the match on the ground

* A person of independent means.
† "Good luck."

and watched, with inexplicably rapt attention, its fading flame against the reddish sand of the path.

It had been warm in Sebastopol, but in Moscow it was cold. It was the month of November, and Maître Rueil was wearing a fur coat. He had tracked down Monsieur Jean very quickly, who turned out to be an uncommonly obliging chap of the old-lecher variety; despite what were in a very literal sense his declining years, he was astonishingly spry, walked with a spring in his step, chuckled, chortled, pinched the maids and talked only of girls and drinking in the convivial company of students. Supposing that Maître Rueil had no Russian, on the very first day he said to the owner of a restaurant in the presence of the maître, with whom he was dining:

"He's French. Don't be too scrupulous when you bring the bill. We can discuss the percentage later."

The owner smiled understandingly. "All the same, don't be too overzealous," coldly interjected the maître in Russian. "*Excusez-moi*," muttered Monsieur Jean. "*C'était une erreur. Je croyais que vous n'entendiez pas le russe*,"* he added with faux naivety. "It's quite all right," replied the maître with a shrug of the shoulders. "I don't blame you." And

---

* "Forgive me. My mistake. I wasn't aware you spoke Russian."

the maître burst into laughter: the thought that Monsieur Jean might take umbrage particularly amused him.

The maître's profound indifference did not impede his immediate evaluation of this man—even prior to the incident in the restaurant. The maître conversed with him monosyllabically; Monsieur Jean fawned and giggled. He did, however, drive the maître around Moscow, showed him a few places where the young man who was the reason for the maître's visit could be found, and, finally, communicated the address of the institution.

"I no longer require you," said the maître on the third day. Monsieur Jean rejoiced, but made a sad face. "Wait, where are you going?" said the maître in sudden exasperation, seeing that Monsieur Jean was getting ready to leave. "Here"—he handed him some money—"take this for your troubles and have a drink with some girls in the company of students." Monsieur Jean smiled and executed a complicated pas with his feet. "Still dancing?" said the maître, narrowing his eyes in contempt. "I don't understand you; you're a hundred years old yet you jump around. You're old bones," he said even more scornfully. "You'll soon snuff it; but you'll even go to heaven with a spring in your step. Well then, avaunt!" Monsieur Jean vanished.

The maître wasted several successive evenings in his searches. He was consumed by a feeling of disgust for everything that he did, and he began to think that the most honourable course of action would be to abort his mission and head home. "I need a rest," thought the maître. "I need a rest." And so he decided that if his visit to Madame Rose changed nothing, tomorrow he would pack his things and leave. Let them give the job to Smirnov. That evening, having donned his black suit, he set out for Madame Rose's institution.

He arrived too early; nobody was there yet. He entered a long, spacious room illuminated by an enormous lamp with a beautiful shade; along the walls soft chairs had been laid out. A ballroom pianist with a dismal Jewish face played some melodies in a minor key. The salon's tone was one of muted misery: sorrowful beauties in black gowns, holding in their hands giant roses that looked more like sunflowers, were hung along the walls; in a massive painting, *The Executioner of Nuremberg*, was depicted a man, bared to the waist, with curiously languid eyes, wielding an axe above the head of a youth queerly reminiscent of Schiller; the youth was being comforted by a buxom lass; fat tears were painted on her cheeks. Maître Rueil was amazed; Madame Rose's salon was nothing more than a bordello.

"*Elle va fort, quand même*,"* he thought.

---

* "She's going strong, all the same."

Little by little the salon filled with guests. They looked to be arriving from a graveyard or a funeral service: the ladies smiled mournfully and never let go of their handkerchiefs.

"*Drôle de p—*,"* the maître told himself: he was beginning to feel puzzled.

Finally, from a side door entered a woman of around thirty in a plunging décolleté gown: this was Madame Rose. The maître recognized her immediately: two years ago in Paris she had been arrested for blackmailing a prominent businessman. She was well known by the clientele of all the fun little spots in Montmartre. They called her L'Hirondelle.† She led a fairly frivolous sort of life: she danced au naturel where it was possible and permissible; she engaged in business of a rather singular nature and very freely eyed a great many things. She also remembered the maître, who had once foretold her death in poverty and every venereal disease. She approached him and, having lifted his chin with her lacquered index finger, imperiously pronounced:

"Ah, you're here as well? Do you see? *J'ai fait du chemin, moi*.‡ Do you recall what you predicted for me?"

---

* "D—n strange."
† The Swallow.
‡ "I've come a long way."

"Yes, clearly I was mistaken where the poverty is concerned," replied the maître.

"*Méchant!*"*

She spoke with him for several minutes before moving off.

The maître was left alone. He felt very odd among this crowd of strange and ridiculous Russian people, with painted ladies slowly waltzing in the red light emanating through the lampshade. The pianist continued to play, growing pale with fatigue and chagrin; several times L'Hirondelle's glistening skin flitted before the maître's eyes. The young man who was the reason for his visit was not there. The maître sat in the same spot for the whole evening. Then, shaking off his gloomy torpor and deciding to send a telegram to Paris the following morning, terminating his mission, he walked out into the street. The lights sparkled in the icy puddles. By a lamp post stood a man in a fur coat, blind drunk. He cried and sang, trailing off and once again, sobbing, beginning: "Misty morn, ashen morn…"† The maître stood beside him awhile and then walked off. The light mist, so like that of the morning in Constantinople when he dreamt of the falling building,

---

* "Wicked man."
† The opening lines from Ivan Turgenev's lyric poem 'V doroge' ('On the Road'), which lent its text to a popular Gypsy romance of the nineteenth century.

began to ring quietly in his ears. "I'm ill," the maître said to himself with a degree of familiarity, but this time he was neither surprised nor afraid.

Suddenly, two paces in front of him he saw a broad-shouldered figure blocking his way. "Excuse me," said the maître; and that instant he heard the voice of the actress with whom he had journeyed aboard the ship. "That's him!" she shouted. Suddenly the maître felt cold and indifferent. Three men threw themselves at him. Warding them off with his left arm and his legs, with his right he extracted a revolver and, already firing at the fiercer of his assailants, recognized in him the youth whose photograph he had been given back then in Paris. But it was too late; the shot rang out and rushed along the windows of the buildings and along the pavement. Just then a hand with brass knuckles came crashing down on top of the maître's head. His eyes floating over the actress's pale face, Maître Rueil lost consciousness.

He came to his senses only three days later. He was lying in a bed in an unfamiliar room. Reaching out his hand laboriously towards the bedside table, he groped at a slip of paper. It was a telegram from Paris: "APPRIS RÉCOMPENSE FÉLICITATIONS CONGÉ TROIS MOIS REVENEZ BERNARD".*

---

* "Learnt recompense congratulations three months leave awaiting you Bernard".

With great difficulty he recalled what had happened to him. A crazed, belated sense of regret gripped him: he saw, as though truly before him, the icy puddles, the actress, the drunkard singing "Misty morn…" and the youth at whom he had directed his revolver. All his life, now changed and unlike that which he had led until then, he would recall that trip to Moscow. And in his diary he jotted down several unexpected lines about a certain variety of seasickness, about the sad meaninglessness of journeys, and about the tear-stained faces of Moscow's prostitutes.

HAPPINESS

(1932)

André Dorin, a pale boy of fifteen, was alone in his parents' apartment in Sainte-Sophie, forty versts from Paris. His stepmother was at Cannes—as always at this time of year—and his father had left for Paris in the morning, warning André not to expect him for dinner: this meant that he would return in the early hours, wake André up and say to him, in his calm, happy voice, which André so loved:

"Are you asleep? Get up and sit with me awhile. First we'll indulge in a little alcoholism, then I'll tell you some fascinating anecdotes."

He would make André don his pyjamas and go through to the dining room; then he would brew some coffee, carefully pour into the cups a few drops of rum and tell André a great many trifles that would seem to him ludicrous and absurd; then he would extract from his brown briefcase a book in a leather binding, hand it to André and add:

"I found this book purely by chance. Do you remember, you were talking about it and saying how much you wanted it? Imagine, I was walking across the Elysian Fields, when I saw an empty car just standing there, and inside it—that same book. I thought: my God, that's the very one my son was telling me about—what a happy coincidence. So I opened the car door, extracted the book, hid it in my briefcase and walked off unnoticed. Can you imagine the luck of it? Only, please, show it to no one. There's even some sort of inscription in it."

And inside the book would be written, in his father's even hand: "*À ne pas lire la nuit, s.v.p.*"*

By force of habit, Henri Dorin, André's father, still thought of his son as a little boy and would speak to him as though he were nine or ten years old. He knew, however, that André was exceptionally mature for his years; he could see this by the books André read, by André's questions and observations, which to him seemed unusual coming from the mouth of his young son, whom he had still recently borne on his shoulders and for whom he was ready to spend hours pulling faces, telling fairy tales and going to such efforts just to make him laugh. But André laughed exceedingly rarely. All the more often Henri

---

* "Not to be read at night, please."

Dorin thought that the older André grew, the more he came to resemble his late mother, his first wife, whom he could never forget. She was nineteen when Dorin met her, although to look at she might have been fifteen. She always wore white dresses, her footsteps were light and soundless, and Dorin would tell her that she was like one of those daytime spectres that were just as rare in the world as white robins. She was very sickly; and although she never complained, except in regard to a heightened sensitivity, Dorin took her to see a renowned professor, who told him that his wife ought to have a child; it would regenerate her entire bodily system. "Would you like to have a child?" Dorin asked her several days after this. She closed her eyes tightly and nodded. Dorin did not know then that it would be a death sentence for her.

On the night of the birth, when a different doctor, looking at him sternly, said that only a madman could hope for a happy outcome—"She's just a girl"—Dorin was beside himself. From the moment when she was brought to the clinic—this happened late at night—until the early hours of the summer's morning he paced around the little square in front of the building in Saint-Cloud where she had been admitted (he feared going inside yet could not leave); on the other side of the glass door, the light shone evenly in the foyer, the building was quiet, everything around was still and uneasy—and this endless waiting dragged on until the morning, when they told him that his wife was dead. He nodded, thrust his hands into his pockets and walked off, forgetting even to ask whether the child had survived; he came to his senses only two days later, having been awoken by a policeman and taken to the commissariat of the Ménilmontant neighbourhood. The policeman said that he had found the man sleeping on a bench and that, since he had no money or documentation on him, he had arrested him for vagrancy.

"What is your surname?" asked the commissioner, turning to Dorin and looking at his soiled, crumpled suit and boots that had split at the seams. Only in this instant did Dorin comprehend that his wife was dead—and for the first time he began to weep.

"You do not want to tell me your surname?" continued the commissioner. "Evidently you have good reason to want to hide it. I understand perfectly."

"You don't understand at all," said Dorin. "My surname is Dorin, I'm no vagrant, nor am I a criminal. Telephone my Paris office and ask for the director."

"Understand that if this is a joke," said the commissioner warily, "you shall have cause to regret it."

Nevertheless, he did telephone the office.

"Monsieur Dorin is with you?" shouted the astonished voice down the telephone.

"He wants to talk to you," replied the commissioner and passed Dorin the receiver. Dorin ordered the car to be sent for him; twenty minutes later the chauffeur was opening the door of the heavy six-seater automobile to the unshaven man in soiled clothing, doffing his cap, bowing and saying, as always:

"*Bonjour, monsieur.*" The commissioner, with a bemused and at the same time satisfied look, waved them off. Having arrived home, bathed, shaved and changed his clothes, Dorin summoned to his room the housekeeper, who told him that *madame* was buried at Père-Lachaise and that his son was in the room allocated to the wet nurse. Only then did Henri Dorin see André for the first time. The boy was very small and weighed only six pounds. "Everything she could give," thought Dorin, "all her fragile strength she gave to this child—and it cost her her life."

It seemed to him then that he would dedicate all his time to his son; the thought that he could marry for a second time did not occur to him, though he was only twenty-six. For many years he lived truly thinking only of his son. However, the more André grew, the more Dorin felt the unconscious, palpable love for his son being replaced by a different feeling, no less powerful, but devoid of that original acuity, when every movement of André's little body had reverberated in his heart. And although he continued to love his son, ostensibly as much as ever before, in recent years he had once again become susceptible to other feelings—and he realized for the first time in all this while that he was still young, rich and, to all intents and purposes, almost happy. André was a clever child, an able student and such a voracious reader that Dorin, who slept exceedingly soundly, bought for himself an alarm clock, which he set for two o'clock in the morning—so that he could wake up and go through to André's room; he would find his son in bed with a book in his hands. "Well, *monsieur*," he would say. "Is *monsieur* still reading?" He would prise the book from André's hands, kiss him on the forehead and leave—and only then would André fall asleep.

Dorin married for a second time when André was fourteen. He had become acquainted with Madeleine quite by chance in a café, where he had stopped for half an hour after breakfast one day. Madeleine was perched opposite him; Dorin observed her elongated grey eyes, which from the first moment seemed moist to him—everyone who so much as glanced at Madeleine had this impression—her red lips and fair hair, so finely and thoroughly curled that it recalled the beards of Assyrian kings. Dorin felt a curious stirring the instant he set eyes on Madeleine. He did not even realize that the source of this was she; suddenly he began to feel as though he had forgotten something exceptionally important, or else had failed to do something of the utmost necessity, or perhaps there had been some tragedy at home: might André be ill? Madeline sat in her seat, stirring a cup of tea long gone cold and glancing from time to time at Dorin, as though unable to decide whether or not to leave. Finally she looked at the clock, summoned the waiter, opened her long, narrow purse, like a black leathern envelope—when suddenly it transpired that the little billfold with money, which ought to have been there, had been forgotten at home. "My God, what's to be done?" she said in a low voice. Upon hearing this, Dorin understood what the source of his anxiety had been. "Allow me," he said after a moment's silence. "No, no, *monsieur*, thank you a thousand times over. It's simply maddening. Heavens, there couldn't be anything more idiotic," she said. In the end, however, she was left with no alternative. They left the café together; Dorin sat Madeleine down beside him, and after this, during the course of a whole evening and into the small hours of the morning, his yellow Chrysler was seen in various quarters of the city, and in the Bois de Boulogne, and on the road to Versailles; it was a June day, and the sultry heat was tempered by a light summer breeze; green leaves danced in the wind, the glass of the car glinted keenly, and the sun's yellow disc skimmed, shimmering, across the black wings of the car.

Sitting beside Madeleine in the car, Dorin subconsciously knew that he could not simply leave this woman. Madeleine knew this even before he did. She told him that she lived alone in Paris, that her parents lived in the Alpes-Maritimes, that she was twenty-eight years old, that she wrote articles on urbanism and sometimes appeared in films. They had a bite to eat on the Grands Boulevards, after which they set out for another drive, then Dorin found himself in Madeleine's apartment; later, as if nothing had happened, he saw, as if in a dream, her shoulders, her breasts with what seemed to him naive, boyish nipples, and her long legs and moist eyes. In the morning, without getting up from the divan, he reached over to the telephone standing on the little side table, rang his number in Sainte-Sophie and told André that he would be home at around four o'clock that afternoon. "All right, Papa," calmly replied André. "I won't be at home then; I'm going out to hunt for butterflies." "Excellent, so we'll see each other after." Half an hour later, in the crepuscular light passing through the shutters, Dorin asked Madeleine to be his wife. "You're mad," she replied, laughing. "I'm not joking," repeated Dorin with a quaver in his voice. Madeleine looked at him earnestly, then she embraced him tightly, kissed him and didn't say a word.

At four o'clock that afternoon Dorin brought her home, to Sainte-Sophie. He gave her a tour of the house and showed her all of the rooms with the exception of André's, which was locked with a key as usual; André would never leave the door open on going out. They went through to the dining room; Madeleine paused by the long mirror fastened to the wall in order to fix her hair. Dorin approached her from behind and embraced her; her lips began to murmur; she, gasping from the tension of his muscles and leaning over, turned to him so as to kiss him, and in that instant spotted someone else's eyes: on the threshold of the room stood a scrawny young boy staring intently at her and Dorin. Dorin blushed, released Madeleine's shoulders from his grip and said in an unexpectedly cheery voice:

"André, allow me to introduce your future new mother. Madeleine, this is my son, André."

"*Alors, mon petit…*" Madeleine began, mistakenly using the same tone of voice that she had just used with Dorin;

apprehending this immediately, she began afresh: "*Mon petit, faisons la connaissance.*"*

André made a low bow, kissed her hand and coldly replied: "*Enchanté, madame.*"†

Ever since the day when Madeleine first crossed the threshold of the Dorins' home, André had sensed some changes in its calm, happy atmosphere. Madeleine brought with her something new and sharply distinct from what there had been before. André disliked Madeleine because everywhere she turned up, everywhere her figure went and her low voice rang out, there invariably reigned a single aura, and everything surrounding her began to acquire a definitive meaning, at the centre of which was she, Madeleine. It was as if she spoke through her presence: "What you think, do or read is important only so long as I'm not here; but the minute I appear, you shall think only of me and consider my proximity the sole purpose of your life." Madeleine did not consciously strive for this, but within her there was a peculiar psychological humidity, a readiness at any moment to accommodate any movement that occurred amid the charged atmosphere. Her lips and hands were always hot, and when in the evening she

* "Well, my boy… Let's get acquainted, little one."
† "Delighted to meet you, madam."

would offhandedly kiss André on the forehead, bidding him goodnight, André felt ill at ease.

Madeleine was marked by a most felicitous physical equipoise, and her body was in a certain sense just as perfect and unwearying as the lungs of an eagle or the muscles of the world's best athlete; any sensation that gave an ordinary person mild pain or satisfaction, the lure of which was easy enough to overcome, stirred up a tempest in her blood. It was as if her senses were a long sword, whose tip, after the blow had already been delivered, still quivered and trembled, fluttering like a banner in the wind, or the white trim of a sail over the rippling sea, or the wings of a bird sitting on the water. Henri Dorin knew this just as well as André, but he thought that it was true only for him, and for no one else; he thought that before meeting him Madeleine had known neither herself nor her senses, which were revealed only in close proximity to him and beyond which there was nothing. His relationship with André had not ostensibly altered in any way, yet Henri Dorin and his son now stood, as it were, on opposing shores of a steaming hot river that separated them and that neither one nor the other could cross.

Henri Dorin was often not at home: he would leave now for Paris, now for the Midi, where his factories were located. Sometimes André would accompany him; trips with his father were the greatest of pleasures for him. He would sit in the car and watch the ornament on the radiator, an Indian head with hair swept back, flying in the wind; the head hurtled along, hovering above the even surface of the asphalt, past houses and trees, along the coastline, down the streets of provincial towns and Paris's boulevards; and in his imagination André had long since thought up the title for a story about the car: 'The Indian Voyager'. The story, however, he never wrote. All the trips ended well; only once did André return from a journey in the car with an enormous bump on his forehead. It happened as André and his father were driving home one evening in Paris—there had been a downpour, and the sides of the road along which they were driving were covered by a thin layer of mud—and the boy's father, hurrying to reach Sainte-Sophie before nine o'clock, pressed ever harder on the accelerator—at the corner of one of the streets in Passy, which was almost deserted at this hour, André suddenly spotted a little fox terrier pup running across the road, directly in the car's path, so there was nowhere to swerve; the street was too narrow. Scarcely able to breathe, André looked at his father and, without time to utter so much as a word, saw that he had also clocked the puppy. However quickly all this was taking place, André still had time to think: What will Papa do? "Hold on, André," was all Dorin said, and that very moment the brakes screeched and squealed, and with extraordinary speed the Indian head began to veer right; the car skidded at full speed. André was thrown out of his seat and hurled into a corner; then he heard a powerful impact, and everything stopped. André stood up where he had landed, and the first thing he saw was the puppy, which had managed to run to the opposite pavement and was wagging its short snub tail. His father's hands settled him in the seat beside him, and in an altered voice he asked:

"That was a close shave, wasn't it, André?"

André didn't know whether to laugh or cry.

"You aren't hurt, are you?"

"No," replied André. "I just have a bump on my forehead."

His father felt his head. "You're made of iron, young man," he said. "Nothing damaged whatsoever. Let's check the car now."

But the car had not suffered either, and the remainder of the journey passed as usual. There was no conversation about the reason for the "catastrophe"; only not far from home, André asked his father:

"Papa, why in fact do they cut fox terriers' tails?"

"Why indeed?" said Dorin. "Perhaps they think they're more comfortable without it, though I find that very doubtful."

"Now, Madeleine," said Dorin as he entered the dining room with André, "only thanks to André's selfless heroism do I have the pleasure of dining at home this evening."

"How so?"

And so Dorin related an absolutely fantastic story about how, at full speed, André had stopped the car "with the help of the auxiliary air brake and the alarm signal"—while he himself had been paralysed with horror and was unable to move a muscle; how a crowd of people had gathered around André and warmly thanked him for this selfless act and how one town councillor, who happened to be there and whose life also, by the way, had been saved by André, immediately proposed that he become an honorary citizen of the district that the councillor had represented for twenty years; and how André had declined this honour and left, accompanied by the people's cries of jubilation, causing his head to swell, which was particularly noticeable in one spot, where the bump had formed, serving as incontrovertible proof that the story corresponded exactly to the truth.

André frowned as he listened to his father's tale; he didn't like it when Dorin spoke to Madeleine about him in such a way—André thought that his relationship with his father ought not to extend to a third party.

André stayed at home more often; he would retire to his room to write, to attend to his beloved butterflies, or to read his books; he was particularly interested in books on zoology. His father was the only person he would on occasion initiate into his activities.

On one of those airless summer evenings when André ran off immediately after dinner, telling Madeleine in that same cold tone he always took with her: "Forgive me, I must dash," Henri Dorin had noticed in the depths of the garden an electric light coming from among the trees. It took him by surprise. He walked over and saw André, who was standing over a hollow glass cylinder illuminated by a modest electric lamp. In the cylinder, slowly crawling over the glass, were two torpid butterflies with large wings. André was examining them closely.

"What are you doing?" asked Dorin.

André explained to his father that for several months he had been keeping in his room the larvae of these butterflies, which were not found within a range of one hundred and twenty kilometres.

"These are female butterflies," said André. "And you'll see, Papa," he continued, raising his head and looking at his father, "that the males, sensing the presence of these females, will fly here—almost one hundred and fifty kilometres."

"Aren't you getting your hopes up a bit much, André?" asked Dorin. "One hundred and twenty kilometres? How? I can understand one, maybe two, or even ten—but one hundred and twenty? André, I'm afraid I don't believe your experiment will succeed."

"You'll see, Papa," said André. "I'll put out the light now and wait here. You go upstairs. I'll call you."

Dorin left. Much time passed; night had already fallen. André had still not returned.

"What's he playing around with in the garden?" asked Madeleine.

"An interesting experiment; here's what it consists of…" And so Dorin told Madeleine.

"Wonders never cease," she said. "What a queer boy," she added, smiling and thinking of something else entirely. Suddenly, from beneath the window came André's triumphant whisper: "Papa, they're here!" Dorin and Madeleine followed André, inadvertently like him, treading on tiptoes and trying not to make any noise. André walked ahead. "I'll turn the light on," he whispered and began waving his hand. "Papa, come here." They drew closer; André switched on the electricity, and Madeleine and Dorin saw on the illuminated glass dozens of enormous butterflies crawling back and forth and beating their wings.

"You couldn't exactly describe it as raucous," noted Madeleine with a laugh. André shot her an angry and contemptuous look.

André spent a lot of time on his own; whenever his father was away from home, he almost never left his room; only on rare occasions would he suddenly appear from the open door to go into Dorin's study in order to fetch some book or other—his appearance would always be unexpected, for he moved about in absolute silence; on account of this, Madeleine would often start when she saw him. "Did I startle you?" André would ask in such instances. "I'm sorry."

The house frequently hosted guests: one time this resulted in unpleasantness for André. At the time, his father had disappeared for a few days; André himself had gone out in the morning, taking with him his butterfly net and a small jar that had a wooden lid with holes drilled in it for air—into this jar André placed newts and water beetles, which he would catch at a little lake about three miles from his house. He was accompanied by his mastiff, Jack—it amused him that Jack would bark at the lizards. André had been walking all day; whenever he grew tired, he would sit down on the ground and lie there with his face to the sun; his eyes closed, he would see a red expanse before him; the earth beneath him hummed; the grass quietly hissed, swaying in the gentle breeze, and beside him he could hear Jack's even breathing—and amid the red expanse, butterflies, the Indian head and other strange, barely recognizable objects would appear and disappear. André got up and walked on. His jar was already full of newts, his legs were covered in scratches; he was tired and it was beginning to grow dark, and the forest in which he now found himself was beginning to emit its nocturnal sounds. "Time to head home, Jack," said André. "Let's go." It was just then that he recalled having neglected to lock his door as he was leaving.

As he approached the house, he saw the lights on in every room, including the lamp above his desk. He bolted upstairs; there was no one in the hallway, and from the dining room he could hear Madeleine's voice. André approached his room; the door was ajar. He pushed it open and saw that his notebook was lying open, novel-like, on his desk. An unfamiliar woman with a pale face and bright-red lips was sitting in his chair. Reclining on the arm of the chair was a young man embracing the woman; his lips were almost touching her ear. André entered so quickly that the young man had no time to alter the situation. He looked at André and said:

"I haven't the pleasure of knowing you, young man, but in future I would advise you to knock before entering." Choked with anger, André was unable to utter a word. Jack began to growl. André suddenly recovered the gift of speech. "*Allez-vous-en*,"* he said quietly.

"What did you just say?" said the young man, rising from the chair. Jack's growling became frenzied. André held him by the collar and repeated:

"*Allez-vous-en, vous et votre dame*. This is my room." Without realizing, André raised his voice to drown out the growling of the dog.

Five minutes later Madeleine knocked on André's door.

"André, you must go and apologize. What's the meaning of this?"

"*Madame?…*" said André enquiringly.

"You must apologize."

André shrugged his shoulders.

"Pray do me the favour," he said in an even voice, as though reading from a book, "of conveying my regrets to *monsieur* and *madame* for what happened."

He leant over his book, pretending to read. Madeleine turned and left. There was silence in André's room. He

---

* "Get out."

rang the bell, was brought something to eat and ate his dinner; after this he lay on the divan and fell asleep.

He awoke during the night, got up and went over to the window. White summer clouds obscured the high moon; the air was warm and still; everything around was quiet. Suddenly in the dining room Madeleine's swooning voice said:

"Do you really?"

"When I visit you," replied a man's voice, "I feel as though I've grown wings."

"Wings of love?" Madeleine intoned again.

Silence descended. Then some movement could be heard, and an infinitely altered female voice, breathless and hurried:

"Have you gone mad?"

André withdrew from the window and sat down in an easy chair. Again, sounds came from the dining room, but André remained indifferent. "Wings of love," he repeated to himself. "Where have I read about wings?"

And he recalled reading about several species of ant, which, during the mating season, grow wings and rise into the air, only then to fall and perish by the thousand. "And then there are the drones," thought André, "who fly after the queen; the weak are the first to be left behind, then others—until only one, the best and the strongest, reaches her. There they are, those wings of love. That's what Madeleine is talking about. But what of Papa?"

André lay on the divan and began to sob.

André sat in his room, writing. He was dreaming of eventually becoming a great writer, like those whose books were published by Grasset and *La Nouvelle Revue Française*, dreaming how, dressed in a black overcoat and a navy suit, with a beret on his head and an Omega watch on his left wrist, he would walk about the Latin Quarter and how someone's impudent voice would say behind him as he went: "*Mais regardez donc, c'est bien André Dorin.*"* While he, without turning, and even quickening his pace in vexation, would walk on. The only thing he was unable to imagine was what exactly he would write. There just wasn't a single subject, among all those to which he had given considerable thought, that he could make work; everything had seemed simple to begin with: open with a description of the main character, then his living conditions, the books he read, then his journey to England and his strange encounter on a foggy London street with yellow lamps—an encounter that would determine his fate—and all this would be written in a single breath, so that having

---

* "Why, look, it's André Dorin."

begun the story, it would be impossible to break away from it. But each time that André reached a crucial point, everything came out so poorly and artificially that he would give up in despair, and with alarm begin to think that he would never make a famous writer of himself. He was unable to concentrate his efforts on a single line of the narrative; as soon as he began describing something, he wanted to say everything he knew about it and begrudged leaving anything out—this gave the impression that he knew nothing about those things that were not mentioned and were truly not required in this story, but which in and of themselves were very important, interesting and the sole intellectual province of the intelligent and observant. When André began to describe London, he would invariably pass over to reflecting on English history and present his verdict on the British national character, backing it up with examples drawn from across the centuries, mentioning Gladstone, Pitt, Shelley and Shakespeare—although not one of these people had the least to do with the story. Then he would return to his hero; but during all this time his hero had managed to change, unwittingly acquiring some English traits, and his whole characterization would have to be reworked. André patiently set about this work—but something would again lead his tale far off on a tangent, and the quantity of pages covered in writing would grow exponentially, while the heroine would never quite manage to emerge from the London fog; and her solitary figure, walking orphan-like down the street, involuntarily aroused such pity in André that he became grieved in earnest, as if she were really a living person—and he would resolve to write about her the very next day; but again he would be distracted, and again nothing would come out. Then André would throw away his work and go into the garden, while in the evening he would sit down to write his diary, where there was no need to invent anything.

On that January evening when André was alone in the apartment, awaiting Dorin's return from Paris, it was cold and deserted outside, no one passed along the frozen road running nearby the Dorins' home, and there was silence all around; only from time to time could the discordant and soon fading barking of dogs be heard, whereupon Jack would lift his enormous head and growl quietly—André sat at his desk until late, thinking and writing in his diary, in which he wanted to describe his father. He penned a lengthy introduction and then began: "Henri Dorin, my father, was born to be happy."

After this line André wrote nothing; he placed his pen on the desk and lapsed into thought. Yes, of course

Dorin had been born a happy person. From no other person had André heard such a calm and jolly voice, to no other did every misery and setback seem so easily solved as it did to his father. André recalled an episode from his childhood, when he had wept bitterly because a complex plan to construct a narrow paved path from an anthill on the edge of a wood to an old gnarled tree stump, covered over in thin little branches with green foliage—this whole plan, after several days' work, proved to be impracticable, since André had forgotten about the stream separating the ants from the tree stump. André would watch as after a downpour the ants would make their way through the mud towards the bank of the stream and then turn back, uneasily moving their feelers. He believed that the ants just had to reach this tree stump—and so he began to build for them a solid path that no rain could imperil. In the pockets of his breeches he carried stones and a hammer; he carried heavy pails of sand, and made a clumsy attempt at a path leading right to the tree stump. Then he sat on the ground and began to cry—and he arrived home with tears in his eyes. "What's the matter, André?" asked his father. André told him what had happened. His father heard him out with a serious countenance, nodded and said: "You're quite right, André, we'll build it yet; after breakfast I'll go with you and we'll work on it together."

It turned out that there was nothing difficult about it; Dorin laid a low bridge over the stream, tamped down the path, and with André's help continued it up as far as the stump. Remains of this path existed to this very day, until this moment when André at last realized how ridiculous his childish plan had been.

Then André fell to thinking about his evening chats with his father, which had begun to happen only recently, and when for the first time Dorin had spoken to him as an adult. Most often it would be the same argument; it would begin with André going to his father to ask his opinion on some historical event or a book he had read. "All right, then," Dorin would say, "tell me what you think about it, and then I'll tell you my impressions."

So André would speak; often he would say what he was writing or planning to write; sometimes it would be a question that dogged him—the question of Madeleine; but he would pose it in such an abstracted formulation that his father could never have suspected that the question had to do with his wife. Yet whenever André mentioned love, Dorin felt simultaneously both ashamed and happy: ashamed because he was married to Madeleine, happy because of the memory of André's mother. Moreover, he would hold back—and only once did he sit André on his knee, as if the boy were eight years old, and say:

"André, do you know how much I love you?"

"Yes, Papa."

"Well, there's one thing you don't know," he said with more emotion than André had ever known from him, "and that's how much you're like your late mother."

For a whole two days after this, Henri Dorin was silent and pensive.

More often, however, these talks would turn out rather differently. With a perspicacity that was strange in a boy so young, André would notice and observe much sorrow in everything around him; and it was namely these things that would usually draw his interest. He found everything brash, gay and exuberantly distasteful. In talking to him like an adult, Henri Dorin—it flattered André very much, and he knew that it flattered him and was angry at himself for this, but he could never overcome the particular satisfaction this brought—would object:

"Well then, André, I understand your point of view. You're saying that everything is dismal and unpleasant. Without even entering into a discussion of that, but simply—factually, if you will—that isn't so. Look, here comes Jack, bounding up to you; isn't he happy to see you?"

"Jack is a dog," replied André.

"André, André," Dorin said reproachfully. "Come now, you're a student of zoology: you mustn't diminish the significance of animals. You must know that in a certain sense Jack is more perfect than you or I."

"Jack doesn't have reason in the human sense," André insisted, "but rather instinct. Instinct is the desire to eat, to breed, to move—it's necessary so that his muscles don't grow weak, that's all. But could a dog really have any idea of what's good or bad?"

"I don't know, I do not know. Perhaps. Say a man falls ill and dies; his dog won't leave his grave for several days and after some time perishes there too, although it was seemingly in perfect health. What instinct is that? But do let's put all that aside. Can you really not imagine a man so infinitely clever, who sees and understands everything —insofar as man's abilities allow—and finds only good in it?"

"No, Papa, no such man ever existed."

"What about Francis of Assisi, André? Naturally, André, there was Francis of Assisi," and Dorin smiled as he would have done at little André when he solved a problem facing the young boy and everything proved simple and remarkably easy. "There, you see. He knew an awful lot and understood everything—and he was eternally joyful; so it is possible. I was right."

"But I cannot be like that," said André stubbornly.

"Because you don't know much. Don't be offended, André. To understand theoretically is one thing: to feel it is another. There are a great many feelings that you don't yet know, my boy. Just you wait, we'll talk about this again in fifty years' time," Dorin began to joke.

"But what if something bad happens, Papa? Like a catastrophe or…"—André paused and then with difficulty continued—"…or you are betrayed by the woman you love." He used such a bookish expression because it was the first time he was talking about this with his father.

"Ah, André, how curious you are. Very well: a catastrophe—what is a catastrophe? If it's death, then it's all over; if it isn't someone's death but a betrayal, then just think what joy awaits you; you are betrayed, and then, in this betrayed state, you shall know all the delights you once knew. It means a life anew. As far as betrayal is concerned… you see, my boy, the woman you love cannot betray you."

"But what if she does?"

"How do you know?"

"Say I've been told."

"It means it's a lie."

"I have incontrovertible evidence: I saw her being kissed."

"It means there were some terrible circumstances that forced her to act in that way—circumstances which you do not know and which entirely exonerate her. And if there are none, it means that you are mistaken: she isn't the woman you love. But that's rare, André, that's the exception. However, here, on this point, I haven't even the right to argue with you, because I know this, whereas you're ignorant. You see, André, you're at a major disadvantage in such questions."

"How's that, Papa?"

"The fact is," said Dorin, with a barely noticeable, gently teasing smile, "that my clever son, who knows everything, is only fifteen years old. *Voilà, monsieur*. Now, goodnight. And, please, don't try staying up reading till morning; I'll still come and stop you. You couldn't have chosen a more tiresome old man."

"Henri Dorin, my father, was born to be happy."

André read over this line once again. It was very late. Jack was asleep with his head resting on one of his paws. "Why hasn't Papa come yet?" André thought with sudden alarm.

He diligently made up his bed, neatly spreading out the sheets, placed a lamp with a green shade on the bedside table, and extracted Stendhal's *The Red and the*

Black from the shelf, a silk bookmark placed at the three hundred and twenty-eighth page; opening the book, he even managed to read:

"*Mathilde croyait voir le bonheur. Cette vue toute puissante sur les âmes courageuses, liées à un esprit supérieur, eut à lutter longuement contre la dignité et tous sentiments de devoirs vulgaires.*"*

His father had still not returned. So André fetched his overcoat and went out into the road; Jack, who had woken immediately, followed him.

For a long time, André stood looking into the darkness, but he could see nothing. The highway, with its little pebbles frozen to the ground, loomed white before André's eyes, vanishing around twenty paces ahead of him, as though silently falling into an abyss. From time to time the trees lining the road creaked and swayed in the wind; it was terribly cold, empty; there wasn't a light to be seen anywhere. Jack gave a long yawn, then he pricked up his ears, but nothing emerged out of the darkness. Suddenly André noticed that Jack's ears had long been standing to attention; the dog's body was straining forward, as if he was undecided whether to run or stand still. Then André

---

* "Mathilde believed she had happiness in her sight. This prospect, irresistible to courageous souls possessed of a superior intellect, had to struggle long and hard against dignity and every sentiment of common duty."

discerned in the distance a barely audible sound, which consisted of the rumble of tyres over the ground and the quiet hum of an engine. André knew that five hundred yards from the house there was a sharp bend in the highway; the noise from the turning wheels was obviously that same sound André had heard. Then far ahead, amid the darkness, two lights appeared, dancing strangely in the air—as if a drunkard were at the wheel, driving in zigzags. André was seized by alarm; he ran towards the headlights; Jack rushed ahead of him, barking. André reached the car, flung open the door and saw his father sitting there, pale, clutching the wheel with his weakened hand in a leather glove. He didn't smile as he always did whenever he saw André—he merely said to him in a broken voice:

"André, I feel very ill. Help me get home."

André struggled to help his father move away from the wheel, and slowly, confusing the brakes and the accelerator, causing the motor to jerk and making Dorin wince in pain, drove him home. He awoke his father's valet, Joseph, and together they helped Dorin upstairs and laid him on the bed. Finding it difficult to utter the words, Dorin said:

"Joseph, wake the pharmacist and get some aspirin and quinine; tell him I have terrible pain just below my chest and have him give you something for this. Go, as fast as you can."

With unceasing alarm André followed his father's every movement. He suddenly began to think that Henri Dorin might die—and when André thought about this, everything around him became so cold and awful that he decided to die right there with his father. Henri Dorin found the strength within him to smile at André.

"It's nothing, André," he said. "I've just caught cold, you see: my head hurts, and I don't feel too well." He neglected to tell André that en route from Paris to Sainte-Sophie he had blacked out several times. "I'll take the aspirin and quinine, sleep it off, and tomorrow morning we'll have a boxing match in ten rounds."

André understood from the line about boxing that his father was in a very bad way. But he did not have time to dwell on this, for at that moment Joseph came in, panting and bearing the medicine.

"Forgive me, *monsieur*, but since the pharmacist was in such a hurry he couldn't find the capsules and so he just put everything you asked for in sachets. Here's the quinine, and here is the aspirin, and here's something for the pain below your chest; the pharmacist said to take a tablespoon and a half."

"Fine, Joseph, you may go."

Turning to André, Dorin said:

"Wait here a moment, André."

After Joseph had gone, Dorin continued:

"Well, there, André, everything's fine. I'll take these medicines and go to sleep. Go and sleep, too, I beg you. Goodnight."

"Goodnight, Papa," André replied in a whisper. But by the time he had reached the door, his father's voice suddenly stopped him:

"André, do you know Madeleine's address?"

"Yes, Papa," André replied, suddenly realizing why his father was asking him this. But so as not to alarm his father or let on that he had guessed, he said: "Why do you ask?"

"I've forgotten." Dorin quickly and artificially smiled. "One hundred and eighty-three or one hundred and ninety-three—the building number, that is?"

"One hundred and ninety-three."

"Thank you."

Returning to his room, André decided not to undress or go to sleep. Again he extracted *The Red and the Black*, sat down in the easy chair and tried to read. But he was unable to read further than "*Mathilde croyait voir le bonheur*"; he understood none of it. He closed the book; an unexpected drowsiness suddenly took hold of him, and he fell asleep.

He awoke with the feeling that something was nudging his knee. He opened his eyes: Jack was standing beside him. All was quiet in the apartment. André stood up on tiptoe and went to see whether his father was sleeping. On entering the room, he saw Dorin lying with his eyes open, staring fixedly ahead of him. It surprised and even hurt André that his father did not so much as glance in his direction.

"Aren't you sleeping, Papa?" asked André. Dorin said nothing. André looked him straight in the eye; his father continued to stare straight ahead and didn't move a muscle. The terrible thought of death entered André's head: he drew back the blanket and placed his ear to his father's chest; it was warm and his heart was beating. He immediately felt much better, as if nothing at all had happened. "Do you feel very unwell, Papa?"

Dorin didn't answer. "He's fainted," thought André. "Though why are his eyes open?" He began to splash water on his father's face. The face didn't flinch or twitch, and his eyes remained open. André was scared.

Dawn was already breaking when Joseph telephoned to summon a doctor from Paris.

Henri Dorin clearly recalled that moment when, having taken the aspirin and what he took for quinine (he was a little surprised that it didn't taste very bitter), he grasped the tablespoon lying on the bedside table, poured in the remedy for the pain below his chest and swallowed it with a sip of water. Thereafter he saw nothing, understood nothing, heard nothing; he regained the ability to think only after the passage of several hours. He was in no pain. "Thank God, it's passed," he told himself and tried to sit up, but could not. "How dark it is in the room," he continued to think. "But I'm still very weak. It must be morning already: how strange that no one's about. I must call André."

Yet he was unable to call André. It was then that he realized his inability to move even his hands and feet; he was unable to speak, to see or to hear. "Am I dead?" he asked himself in terror. "No, I can't be: surely I wouldn't be able to think. I'm paralysed."

He again lost consciousness.

He knew that there were people moving around him, opening and closing shutters, that night had replaced day—yet he saw, heard and felt nothing. He made an incredible effort to raise his arm, but nothing came of it. Finally his right hand slightly twitched.

This happened on the third day after the evening when he took the medicine. For three days and nights he lay there supine, like a living cadaver; he was moved several times, the doctor gave him injections, but Dorin's body remained motionless. Summoned by a telegram from André, an anxious Madeleine arrived on the evening of the second day and never left Dorin's bedside. Nothing would compel André to leave the room: for hours he would sit on his father's bed, repeating all the while "Papa, Papa", as though hoping that his voice would rouse Dorin out of his terrible unbeing. The doctor informed André that his father had taken an accidental overdose of quinine and it was too early to predict the outcome.

André was the first to notice his father's hand twitch. He fetched a pencil and some paper, but however much he tried to place the pencil in his father's hand, Dorin's fingers would unclench and nothing would come of it. Finally, towards evening, pausing and dropping the pencil, which André would replace in his hand, in shaky letters Henri Dorin wrote: "I can't see, hear or feel anything."

From that point began his recovery. The following morning Dorin was able to move both of his hands; a day later he could bend his knees. After three days, he heard Madeleine's footsteps as he awoke. He recalled how, as a first-year student at the *lycée*, he would amuse himself by clasping his hands tightly over his ears and then, when he removed them, immediately hear a loud rushing noise. So was it now: an odd silence suddenly gave way to various sounds and voices—André, Madeleine, the doctor, Joseph and other people. Then he began—albeit with great difficulty—to speak. The first thing he uttered were the words:

"Get André."

"I'm here, Papa," came André's voice.

"Were you very afraid, my boy?"

"Yes, Papa," replied André, unexpectedly choking and beginning to weep.

That same day the doctor, having summoned Madeleine, spoke with her for half an hour, concluding with assurances of a complete recovery of Dorin's health. "But I'm afraid," he added after a moment's silence, "that he will remain blind for ever."

And so Henri Dorin was blind. At first he, like everyone around him, believed that his vision would return gradually, just as his hearing and his ability to move his arms and legs had done; but while his strength had long since been restored, his vision did not return. He continued to see nothing, and only slowly and nervously did he become accustomed to the constant darkness in which he now lived. What he couldn't see was at first a great obstacle to his moving around; he found it difficult to walk about not because he was blind, but because the muscles in his legs felt weak. He lost his sense of balance; his movements were uncertain; and when he fell, it was always particularly unfortunate, for he wouldn't manage to break the fall by reaching out his arms. It was as if some sort of spring had been extracted from him, one that previously made his body agile and created a natural resistance to all external jolts and collisions. Later he would develop a different manner of walking and moving and an unerring sense for obstacles that stood in his way, which he imagined as dark walls in front of closed eyes. He would no longer knock into stools, tables or armchairs; he would find the door with ease—since there was less of a draught by an open door than by the wall. Several weeks passed and already Dorin could make his way about the entire house with the assurance of a seeing person. Only then did everything, with astonishing speed, begin to change in his perception.

Until now, Dorin had given almost no thought to the misfortune that had befallen him. It was terribly difficult for him; he knew that all that had happened was awful; but he considered his loss of vision a mere physical defect, distressing and lamentable, but nothing more. Like a child, he was gladdened by the thought that he had managed to do everything in life that was essential—like a man who, upon espying a threatening cloud before a tempest sets in, takes shelter in a safe place; he was safe, he had his beloved son and a wife—what did he have to fear?

Yet with each passing day he noted that all this was changing, and that André and Madeleine were involuntarily becoming estranged from him. This first revealed itself on the day when Madeleine led him out for a walk. He falteringly made his way along the highway as she held his arm; it was an almost breezeless spring day.

"What a breeze, Madeleine!" said Dorin.

"You must be joking, Henri—there's no breeze; in fact it's quite astonishing. I was just about to mention it."

"You all…" Dorin suddenly began with exasperation, which Madeleine was quite unaccustomed to. "You all evidently think that if I'm blind, then it must mean that I've regressed into childhood or become an idiot. I can't see anything, true enough, but I feel a strong breeze."

"But I assure you, Henri, that it's all in your mind."

Dorin fell silent and did not initiate any further conversation. On returning home, he sat down on the divan and lapsed into thought for a long time. Everything was quiet at home. Dorin heard the springs in Madeleine's armchair creak, heard her turn the pages of the book she was reading; he heard André writing in his room, and from the fact that his pen would frequently pause and then race across the paper Dorin understood that André was writing a story of some sort—a first draft. Below, automobiles passed along the highway: first there was a Bugatti, then a Hispano-Suiza; then came a 40-cv Renault, followed immediately by a Packard—Dorin identified them infallibly by the sounds of their engines.

In addition to the fact that Dorin's hearing and sense of touch had acutely sharpened—which was, in itself, not surprising—and that everything around him ceaselessly rustled and rang—the darkness before his eyes was full of sounds and saturated with motion that never let up for a single instant—in addition to all this, something new and inconceivable began to reveal itself to him.

Not only could he sense someone's presence in the room, but he could also tell for certain whether the person beside him was calm or angry, happy or sad; every shade and nuance of his state of being suddenly became apparent to Dorin. It was as if a warm breeze emanated from every person, and from this Dorin could tell whether he was weak or strong, what state of mind he was in. One morning, when Madeleine came into the room after he had just finished dressing himself, he sensed her desire before she had managed to utter a single word; before, he had been able to tell by the expression on her face, or by the intonation in her voice, or by some movement of her body or her hands. Now he saw none of this; but Madeleine had not even the time to say anything to him, and before she could utter her usual *"Bonjour, Henri"*, he anticipated her and said:

"Good morning, Madeleine. So, you haven't stopped loving me, then?"

"You can tell?"

"I felt it. Only don't cry."

Madeleine's face, her cheeks moist with tears, appeared right beside Dorin's.

"Henri," she said in a frightened whisper, "I'm afraid when you touch me. Your fingers are different—it feels like someone else's hand is stroking my body. You have new hands, Henri," she said with horror in eyes, which Henri heard in her voice.

"Silly thing," he said tenderly. "You forgot that I'm blind."

Myriad trifles vexed Dorin. Foremost—the inability to read, then the constant and insulting obligingness of all those around him, among whom only André understood that to be overly considerate of his father, and to treat him as one gravely ill, would be to underscore inadvertently his terrible defect. From some things that Dorin said, André realized that his father had correctly divined and appreciated his delicacy.

When left alone, Dorin would begin to recollect. Before, he would rarely tax his memory; what had happened to him was sufficient to take up all his attention. Now, not yet having quite accustomed himself to living in the dark, in which so much had hitherto seemed hostile and alien, he picked over in his mind all his visual impressions and recalled his whole life.

He recalled the cirrus clouds in the dawn sky on the morning when his first wife had died, the glint of automobile windows and their reflections of Madeleine's reclined head, the glitter of the sea along whose bank his Chrysler raced, and André's pale face with his deep-blue, almost feminine eyes; he recalled how, bouncing along, stones would go flying from the road, how scraps of paper would be blown along by the gust of wind; how night fell and in the far-off distance, almost as far as the darkness now, but incomparably more gentle, lights would appear in the air, now high up, now low down; how the beam of the headlights would glide along the dark highway; how, coming out of the final turn, vespertine Paris would reveal itself, all studded in lights, above its centre a red neon glow; how the water in the woods gleamed, how the trees were reflected in the river; how in the ocean there sailed multistorey liners with luminous portholes; how white the soft seaside sands glittered, when as a boy he would return from a swim—how the lighthouses shone, visible far out at sea. Thousands of insignificant and trivial details came rushing back to him: Jack's odd, dancing gait as he bounded up to a St Bernard they met in Paris; the motion of the muscles under his sleek skin; how the reddish tail of a fox flashed when Jack lunged at it one day as they were taking a stroll somewhere in Normandy. Then he saw the streets of Paris, full of people—under the streaming, glistening rain; the flashing green and red lights at street corners; the far-distant, slow-moving sky above his head, the deep-blue ice of northern lakes—and the stifling yellow clouds of dust on France's innumerable roads that year when the war broke out and he and his classmates had slowly journeyed to the front at night on a lorry with blacked-out headlights. "Where are they now?" Dorin wondered. "Mortier was killed in the August of sixteen. What about Bernard?" Dorin recalled how Bernard would speak with his gloomy appearance:

"No, my friends, I know for a fact: I'll be killed on the day the war ends."

He would say this every day and bored everyone with it so much that Mortier, letting fly, said to him one day:

"*Non, mais crève donc et que la guerre finisse!*"*

"How jittery Bernard was before he died," Dorin continued to think. "When was it? A month before the armistice. Yes, Bernard was wrong about the date."

Again he imagined a long and happy life. There he was, returning home after the thunder of shelling, the trenches, machine-gun fire; he still dreamt of the war, but he now lay in a clean bed with cool sheets, in the knowledge that all these horrors, and death, and hunger were behind him, and in front of him was wealth, health, happiness and everything worth regretting later in old age.

Once, when Madeleine came into his room, he could tell by her quick and moreover indecisive step that she wanted to ask him about something of which she was not quite sure he would approve. Madeleine sat down beside him and talked of domestic things; then she asked:

"André, would you have anything against my inviting some guests round?"

Dorin suddenly felt extraordinarily sad. He recalled how, as a child, he would be left at home as a punishment—

---

* "Well, die, then, and let the war be over!"

everyone would go out and he would be left alone in that enormous apartment, scarcely holding back the tears. Yet he replied:

"Of course, Madeleine, of course. Only I won't come down to meet the guests, I'll stay in my room: you can tell them that I've gone away. All right?"

"No, no," Madeleine protested, "you should be there with us."

"That's impossible," Dorin insisted. "I won't. But you must invite the guests, otherwise I'll be hurt."

"As you wish," Madeleine said with a sigh.

And so in the evening the guests arrived. Dorin sat on a chaise longue by the window; the setting sun shone on his blind face, then its warm light slowly declined ever lower—and ultimately darkness fell. Dorin stayed by the window and remained seated on the chaise longue. He could hear—for the window in the dining room was open—the guests discussing him, asking Madeline about his health, her replies. On a sudden, the sound of her voice struck him; he began to listen more attentively. But Madeleine's subsequent rejoinder was made not to the man in conversation with whom her intonation had so struck Dorin. He waited for her again to speak to this man. Five minutes later a male voice asked:

"And how is Henri getting on?"

"Thank you," replied Madeleine, "very well. He's in Paris today."

It was that same intonation: there was no mistaking it. In an instant, Dorin felt as though he were suffocating. But he recovered his senses: having slowly moved the chaise longue away from the window, he migrated to the divan, lay back on the cushion and did not stir again the entire evening. Still he listened—almost mechanically, almost unconsciously—as Madeleine played the piano, as somebody talked loudly about Clemenceau, but now nothing for him existed, apart from her distorted voice. Dorin could not be mistaken in the meaning of this alteration. What he might earlier have ascribed to his imagination was now so clear to him, as if he were seeing everything with his own eyes. Madeleine had spoken in that tone of voice only with him—and only in moments of physical intimacy. How well he knew that voice of hers—with its sudden slight huskiness and uneven breathing! "And yet I'm blind," thought Dorin and vacantly repeated the phrase: "Yes, and yet I'm blind."

Late that same evening—although the guests had not yet departed—the main door opened below and in came André, who went directly up to his room. Dorin heard André approach the window—then retreat, make several quick steps about the room and sit down in the easy chair, but immediately stand back up and again begin to pace around quickly. Half an hour later, he lay down in bed and seemingly fell asleep, for not a sound now emanated from his room.

Until recently, Dorin had spared no thought for whether life was good or bad in broad terms; he would only discuss this in his debates with André. He would say that in life there was more happiness than sorrow, since he himself had experienced happiness more often than sorrow; yet when he was forced to provide proof of his views—and since he was unable to say, "Look here, I live happily, and that is proof enough of what I say"—he resorted to examples drawn from all that he knew or had read. That life was good, however, was, to him, self-evident, without the need for any examples. He was forever grieved, listening to André, and would even say so to Madeleine.

"What a pity," he would say, "that André doesn't take after me. The child is much too morbid, he thinks and reads too much—it's bad for him, Madeleine, don't you think?"

Madeleine would agree with him; André had always remained a stranger to her. She did not know or understand the world of eternally dynamic thoughts, images and revelations that André inhabited; for this she was too healthy and too much a woman. Henri Dorin's happiness was not blind, he was not like Madeleine; within him was some happy combination of physical and spiritual faculties that allowed him to understand both André and Madeleine simultaneously.

"They are both right," thought Dorin, "but when all's said and done, I am more right than they."

And so now the question of who was more right presented itself to him with extraordinary force. In going blind he had been deprived of half the riches he possessed; yet on that evening, when Madeleine had received the guests, he lost something important and very precious—only André remained. Nothing, it seemed, however, could re-establish or replace the feeling that had been destroyed by those few intonations—and this was infinitely sad.

Dorin said nothing to Madeleine; yet from that day on, he felt as if the air that he had so loved, when he had been sighted and happy, the air of his apartment, which constantly surrounded him everywhere he happened to be, like a recurring reminder or a powerful smell of the same perfume—that this air was saturated with alarming and sorrowful things of whose existence Dorin had previously known nothing.

One day he heard downstairs, in the courtyard, a loud squeak—he was told that it was a rat being caught in a trap: Dorin imagined its squashed stomach and he began to feel ill. Another time he could hear the frenzied clucking and squawking of a chicken that Joseph was slaughtering; Dorin heard the beating of its wings as it, now beheaded, ran a few steps about the courtyard; and all this, to which Dorin would have paid no attention previously, weighed uncommonly heavy on him now and made his situation even more oppressive. Each day it became more and more sorrowful for him to think that dusk was falling—as if the setting sun left him in even greater darkness than that in which he now found himself. The far-off sound of a bell, the horn of a passing and retreating automobile, the wind before a storm, the chiming of the clock, and those unfathomable nocturnal sounds whose meaning, no matter how much he tried, he could never understand—all this seemed to him a new and sorrowful revelation. "So everything I knew before was just an optical illusion?" thought Dorin. It seemed strange to him that he had seen Madeleine's eyes, embraced her body, and yet, in those same seconds, had not been able to hear beside him in the air the ringing, the moving, the creeping, the dying away of all these sorrowful sounds, all this final, fatal melody, which continuously sounded around him—and which absolved everything; which was so dreadful that in comparison with it blindness, sickness and betrayal were incidental and nothing more. "What of my happy life?" he continued thinking. He was astonished that he had neither known nor seen this before. "Surely I was no more foolish than others and no less sharp than they; why should it be that what André knew, unable to prove it, but unerringly intuiting it—and his mother knew it too—why should this have remained obscure to me?"

All of a sudden he recalled his conversation with André about the catastrophe. "Yes, then I was saying that after the catastrophe the world would appear altered and full of new delights." Where were they, these new delights?

From that point on, Dorin became grave and taciturn; and Madeleine told one of his friends that Henri had evidently only now fathomed the entire sense of his misfortune.

After Dorin started to consider his new perception of the world, he involuntarily began to avoid André. His fatherly affection had not altered, but those long conversations with André had now come to an end. He unconsciously steered clear of André, because he no longer held that firm and happy conviction that everything was all right, the one with which he previously had been able to counter all André's pessimistic arguments; he would have been compelled to agree with his son, which was utterly inadmissible for a variety of reasons. First, he was the father; secondly, if Dorin were to concede that his son was right, the happiness that André found in the calm, constant certitude of his father would vanish. For André, everything was turning out wrong and dismal—but there was one spot that remained unscathed and was situated beyond misfortune, upset and sorrow—his father. What would have become of André if he had been deprived of this too? Thus thought Dorin—while André was distressed and could not understand why his father was avoiding him.

One day Dorin, overcome by a strange drowsiness, fell asleep after luncheon and dreamt. He dreamt of a river. Infinitely wide, covered in foaming waves, it was barring his way: in the distance he espied its opposing shore, full of vibrantly green trees. "I've recovered," Dorin thought in his dream. "How clearly I can see the water and these trees. I simply have to swim." He stepped into the river; the bottom immediately retreated from under his feet, and he began slowly swimming towards the other bank; a strong current kept dragging him down. In the middle of the river, his strength began to desert him. He looked up—high above was an infinite sky, and in it were stars, although all this was happening during the day. "How strange that I can see stars," Dorin told himself, then thinking that his vision must have come back to him acutely sharpened and that was why he could see even stars by day. Still he swam, yet he was growing more and more tired. He wanted to turn back, but somebody's voice said to him:

"Just don't turn back, just don't turn back."

"Very well," he replied, "but I haven't any more strength."

"You have," said the voice; and Dorin immediately felt lighter. Still, he swam for a long time until he reached the other shore and sat down on the green grass. Everything around him sparkled in the sunlight. He turned his head and saw someone's laughing, uncommonly familiar and uncommonly joyful eyes: "Who is it?" he asked and awoke. It was already evening. Dorin walked over to the window; the darkness standing before him became gentle and tender, a warm evening air surrounded him. From the dining room he could hear Madeleine's deep voice saying to André:

"André, don't you think we ought to wake your father?"

André's voice replied without its usual cloaked enmity:

"Yes, it's probably time."

"I'm not asleep," said Dorin from his window. "How fine everything is," he managed to think. "But why? Just moments ago I understood it all quite differently. What has changed? A single dream? No, it can't be." And, with a smile on his blind face, he went through to the dining room. At dinner he began for the first time to joke with André and laugh—and he felt everything come to life around him. Sombre André began to laugh, Madeleine's voice detached itself from her and surrounded Dorin, and in it resounded those same intonations that there had been that evening when Madeleine had received guests; however, Dorin did not recall this.

Madeleine left him in the early hours of the morning with an abrupt, heavy gait. Henri Dorin was left alone. "What else have I understood?" he enquired of himself. "Right enough, I hadn't heard of or known many sorrowful things and I was happy. But now that I do know them, am I truly any less happy? No, only one must endure this," he thought, almost falling asleep. "One must understand," he forcefully told himself, "that it's all immaterial: catastrophe, betrayal; yes, André was wrong; I'll tell him about this tomorrow. What's important is that I'm alive, that I think and do everything I please—and there, from afar, some cloud of happiness reaches me, one that since childhood has soared behind me—and it envelops me and those dear to me; and against its happy mists everything is impotent, and everything is comic and superfluous; while what I have is infinite and joyous, and nothing is capable of taking that away from me. I'll have to tell André about this, I just mustn't forget it," he said after one final effort—then he drifted off. The dawn was already breaking, the stars had already paled; and there was both light and darkness, ever separate and ever present.

DELIVERANCE

(1936)

Deux verbes expriment toutes les formes que prennent ces deux causes de mort: Vouloir et Pouvoir... Vouloir nous brûle et Pouvoir nous détruit...[*]

HONORÉ DE BALZAC,
LA PEAU DE CHAGRIN

Alexei Stepanovich Semyonov, an engineer and a man of most impressive means, passed, as usual, a half-sleepless night, woke definitively around eleven o'clock in the morning and again, with disgust, thought that these moments of awakening were the most wretched of his life. His head was heavy, there was a bitterness in his mouth, his nose was blocked, and Alexei Stepanovich sensed the taste of the air change as he swallowed it down and then exhaled it poisoned. His eyes ached and itched, his breathing was laboured, and he was tormented by

---

[*] Two verbs encompass all the forms that these two causes of death may take: to Will and to Be Able... Willing burns us, and Being Able destroys us.

heartburn, which had begun many months ago and only rarely eased off for a few hours at a time.

He cast off the bed sheets, lowered from the bed his bloated white feet with their sporadic distended veins and cold sallow soles, inspected the hairy paunch hanging over his thighs, ran his hand along the sides of his head, where just above his ears grew a light fluff, stood up, fumbled around for his slippers and immediately felt that familiar dull ache in his groin. Having made several movements, he began to sweat, like a man coming out of the water, then made his way to the bathroom.

In the apartment, as always, it was quiet. Everything was pristine, everything glittered—the parquet, the lacquered table in the hallway, the mirror affixed to the wall; the bathtub sparkled just as much as everything else. In the hallway there were great white flowers, the name of which was unknown to Alexei Stepanovich; he did not care for flowers and was unable to distinguish them. "An unnecessary business," he muttered as he passed.

Then began his lengthy toilette. First he would clean his teeth with two brushes—one of Indian rubber, the other ordinary—then he shaved, taking an endless time soaping his cheeks and wincing from the razor's touch on his face, and then, finally, took a bath, after which he would begin to freeze and shiver every time; the shaggy dressing gown in which he would wrap himself up would quickly become damp and disagreeably cold. Alexei Stepanovich would remove it and don another. And so, in his dressing gown, he made his way towards the parlour, sat down in an easy chair with a morbid sigh, reached out his hand to a little side table and rang. That very moment the maid came in, bringing coffee. He took a sip and asked:

"What is the weather like today?"

"I'm afraid it's raining again, sir."

"Marvellous," said Alexei Stepanovich.

This meant that today, as yesterday and the day before, he would again be soaked during the daily walk that the doctor had prescribed him. "You must, Alexei Stepanovich," the doctor would say, "otherwise, you know, at our age… one has to take one's health seriously… our body requires… you know, there are certain, as it were, physical requirements…" Alexei Stepanovich disliked that the doctor was talking of *their* age—he was ten years Alexei Stepanovich's junior and enjoyed enviable good health. Alexei Stepanovich had long known by heart everything the doctor was saying. Only he could not fathom what benefit there could possibly be in his walking, squelching through cold, muddy filth, for half an hour each morning; yet he did this obediently, and it was not without a certain malign joy that he noted no improvement whatsoever as a result.

What was most galling, however, was that Alexei Stepanovich was, essentially, not at all ill. Several doctors, having reached a consensus, explained to him that he had no malady in the strict sense of the word, but that the vital functions of his body lacked sufficient intensity; this could be explained, in the first instance, by fatty deposits taxing his heart and, in the second, by his age and general fatigue. However, losing weight was also out of the question, for the means of losing weight also caused a weakening of cardiac function. It was also observed that he had a less than impeccable liver function and a slowing of the blood's circulation, but none of this posed even the slightest danger to his life for the time being, just as the most agonizing sciatica or the at times absolutely unbearable rheumatic pains did not, for example, pose any danger to his life. "But it is beyond question that you must take good care of yourself." Taking good care of oneself meant going to bed early, not drinking, not eating too much, lest there arise some malady in the strict sense of the word—that is, a process that would lead first to a weakening of the body, then to death. Alexei Stepanovich had no fear of death per se; yet the prospect of a slow demise and of the long agonies accompanying it horrified him. With time, however, everything became easier and easier to bear: he now found drink loathsome, his appetite had nearly vanished, and in the early hours of the evening he began to incline towards sleep, though well he knew that were he to lie down, surrendering to this deceitful desire, sleep would elude him all the same.

Having dressed, he went. A fine winter drizzle was falling, there was a wind, and on the avenue du Bois-de-Boulogne there were very few pedestrians. Two identically dressed, broad-shouldered men, neither wearing a hat—athletes to all appearances—walked past Alexei Stepanovich. He watched them go, took several quick steps, but immediately again the pain in his groin and in the small of his back started, and he stopped in his tracks before slowly continuing on. A cold spray hit his face. Having upturned his collar and pulled down his hat, he reached the entrance to the Bois de Boulogne, then turned back and began the ascent home. Through his spectacles, bespattered with rainwater, he vaguely caught sight of his secretary's small, dark-blue automobile, which had drawn up to his apartment a few moments before him.

The secretary was the son of an old classmate, whom Alexei Stepanovich recalled as a boy in shorts and who now lived in Paris and concerned himself solely with the matter of where he might acquire money for wine. Over the last decade, Alexei Stepanovich had seen his friend sober only once, at his daughter's funeral; even then, directly after the service, he, having broken away from the others, stopped off at a café, and when five minutes later he caught up with Alexei Stepanovich, who was leading his wife by the arm, he found he was again drunk, as always. All these years he had lived, never marking or understanding anything, in a ceaseless drunken haze; he would tell, regardless of whether anyone was listening to him, endless tales about himself in the third person, which in recent times were becoming less and less substantive—as his reason waned—and consisted all the more in exclamations. "Alyosha, do you recall?… Colonel Suslikov"—his surname was Suslikov—"would ride out… There was no other mount like it, Alyosha! Colonel Suslikov would ride out. Yes… There was no other mount like it! Fellows! Do you recall, Alyosha?… Yes, if I'm to tell the whole thing, Alyosha, you know… You know me, Alyosha…" Yet from his tale, which could go on for a whole hour, the only clear point was that Suslikov had been a colonel and that at some point he had ridden a horse—no more. His wife, Marya Matveyevna, who for many years during those difficult and hungry times had been Alexei Stepanovich's lover, and her son tried to stay somewhat aloof from him, long having lost hope of reforming him—and so he was left alone and yet still persisted in telling himself his drunken and nonsensical tale. He had spent years on the battlefield, had been a brave and a fine officer; however, having found himself abroad, he immediately took to drink from despair; he would give it up and set to work, but then he would succumb to it once again. They had lived in terrific, incredible poverty, and Alexei Stepanovich had been unable to help them, for he himself got by only with the greatest of efforts—that is, until one day he grew rich, as in a fairy tale or a dream. However, he did not like discussing the source of his wealth, though there was nothing dishonest about it. He had invented an automatic device for a special system used in railway-carriage latrines, which had enjoyed extraordinary success and brought him millions. In those first days, he simply could not accustom himself to wealth, gave away much of his money, helped dozens of people who later dubbed him an imbecile on account of this, which he heard on perfectly good authority from others who were yet to receive any money from him and in every possible way tried to besmirch those who had succeeded in this better and earlier than they. It was then that the Suslikov family began to live well and their boy started attending the best *lycée*; but Alexei Stepanovich gradually felt more and more uncomfortable in their home, for, despite his close relationship with Marya Matveyevna, he was conscious that everything had changed; and the reason for these changes, which were not supposed to have taken place, consisted in his wealth. These changes had been so unexpected and grave that on occasion Alexei Stepanovich was given to musing that, perhaps, it would have been worth renouncing his wealth or being blind to it. He recalled how one day, only a few months before his sudden enrichment, he had entered the Suslikovs' apartment and saw Marya Matveyevna with a rag, mopping up a stain on the floor from a spilt cup of tea; having made a false move, she fell—awkwardly, heavily and painfully. He dashed over to help her up, but she just sat there on the floor and cried. He was kneeling beside her in the uncomfortable, intermediate pose of a man who ought to help someone up and doesn't. "Alyosha," she said, "why all these torments? What crime have I committed?" He had tears in his eyes, he said nothing, and he stroked her hand and looked at the coarsened skin of her fingers, now red from the cold water. From the neighbouring room came the sound of her husband's murmuring—only individual words and short phrases were discernible: "No, Your Excellency, forgive me… I won't allow… I respect… Fellows!"

"There's no bread at home, he sent the boy out this morning to get wine on credit," said Marya Matveyevna, sobbing. Alexei Stepanovich had six francs; he gave them to her, forgoing cigarettes, and half an hour later, when they were taking tea, she said, quite calm now: "Well there you have it, Alyosha, when you become rich, we'll start living the good life. You won't forget us, will you?"

Yet after the passage of only several months, Marya Matveyevna was unrecognizable. The expression in her eyes had changed, having become alarmingly tender, the skin on her hands had paled, by a miracle the wrinkles on her face had vanished, and later still Alexei Stepanovich met her in the street completely by chance in the company of some doubtful specimen of middling years, who was holding her by the waist.

"What's the meaning of this?" Alexei Stepanovich later asked. She regarded him for a long time and replied:

"It means, my dear friend Alyosha, that I am thirty-nine years old and want to live. Now do you understand what it means?"

"Do you think this is fair?"

"*Je m'en f—,*"* she replied in French. "What do I have? A drunken madman, and you, of whom I no longer have

---

* "I don't give a d—n."

any need, you come once a month. I have money, your money. Who has the right to forbid me anything? You know I've paid heavily enough for the pleasures I can now claim."

"You know best, of course," said Alexei Stepanovich. "I make no accusation; I truly have no right to do so. Forgive me."

They sat in her apartment; the grandfather clock ticked away, while at its base lay a black marble leopard—and on the monies that were very likely paid for this clock the family could have lived, in former times, for two months. Alexei Stepanovich sighed, kissed Marya Matveyevna's hand and left.

Marya Matveyevna's son had graduated from the *lycée* and was studying at university; he would sometimes visit Alexei Stepanovich, who would be amazed by how much this young man of frail aspect could eat. He later decided that Anatoly ought to do something besides his university studies and appointed him as his secretary; but all this was merely a pretext, and Alexei Stepanovich's real aim was to see Anatoly as often as possible. Several times a week Anatoly would come by automobile, which, according to Alexei Stepanovich's wishes, had been placed at his disposal for matters of business, and he would tell him about the letters he received in various languages and which almost always contained some appeal for help. Anatoly was the only person whom Alexei Stepanovich still loved. It was uncertain whose son he was—Suslikov's or Alexei Stepanovich's. Marya Matveyevna, in various periods of her life and depending upon her mood, would now tell Alexei Stepanovich, "Don't forget you have a son," and now remind him, "Remember that this child bears no relation to you whatsoever." Anatoly had been born in Russia, and now there was no way to recall or clarify the matter. But even this was immaterial. Wealth had no effect on Anatoly. He loved books, libraries and music, and nothing else interested him; he was a little naive, honest and forthright. Only with Anatoly would Alexei Stepanovich still joke and feel at ease, escaping for a few hours that feeling of unvanquishable disgust for everything that filled his life and about which neither he nor the doctors ever spoke a word, although it was precisely this question that was most essential and most dreadful.

Alexei Stepanovich chatted with Anatoly for half an hour, suggested that he stay to lunch, joked, and it seemed that the dark mood that had possessed him since morning had lifted somewhat. After lunch, however, it gained ground when an engineer by the name of Uralsky showed up with his latest wife.

The engineer Uralsky was a man of around forty, plump and full of *joie de vivre*, a glutton and a cheery conversationalist. Whenever he stopped joking and spoke in all earnestness, it became apparent that he was well educated, very understanding and no fool. He was, however, distinguished by an excess of affection, was forever marrying and divorcing—for the fourth time already in as many years—and in each of his wives there was something strange, something that united them despite their difference in age, hair colour, height and dimensions, the smack of some cheap and undoubtedly foreign demi-monde—so that an outsider would have the impression that these were all the same woman, possessed of a great, though not inexhaustible, gift for transfiguration. Yet the most astonishing and lamentable thing of all was something else—namely, that in the presence of a beloved woman Uralsky would turn into a complete fool, and to elicit a positive response apropos of any business matter would be impossible. He would mumble, smile inanely, gaze at his beloved woman; he would lose all his wit and acumen and make of himself a pitiful and repugnant spectacle.

He had brought his new wife in order to introduce her to Alexei Stepanovich. She had a rather wide posterior, great black eyes, unnaturally devoid of human expression, bright-red lips and copper hair. Alexei Stepanovich kept trying to recall where he had seen such eyes before; he made a supreme effort and remembered that it was in the Berlin zoological garden, by the railing of that grotesque species of antelope that bears the name "gnu".

The conversation was stilted; moreover, Uralsky's wife knew no Russian, and so Alexei Stepanovich had to muster his French, which he abhorred, for he would have to strain his attention and, against his wishes, utter things he had never thought and which he would never ordinarily have said, had the conversation taken place in Russian. As Uralsky was leaving, Alexei Stepanovich lost his temper and asked:

"Wherever do you dig these people up?"

Of late he had grown accustomed to speaking candidly with people, and what he would never before have let slip from his mouth now came out easily and naturally; now people could no longer take offence at him because, as Alexei Stepanovich knew perfectly well, it was not to their advantage. However harshly he spoke to them, his company would always turn it into a joke; and this was the first observation that caused him to wonder whether he had been mistaken his entire life in supposing that certain things were good and others bad, agreeable or disagreeable, offensive or inoffensive.

He opened the newspaper, read several lines and lay it aside, continuing almost unconsciously to mull over those same questions that had entered his head several years ago and since which time had given him no rest. When he was poor, there had been no time to think about abstract things: he had to get money, roam the streets, beg, sit for hours, waiting for those people on whom his regular income of several hundred francs depended—and on this he expended all his time and energy. Later, however, once all this had stopped and when Alexei Stepanovich—after a chaotic month during which alternated, with hitherto unseen variety, impressions, sensations, people and business—was left alone for the first time in his new apartment, and when, it seemed, he really did have nothing to envy, he felt a sense of ennui and emptiness in his soul; and thereafter it never left him, and so too his numerous ailments, which had essentially existed prior to this, but which, from a lack of time and money, he had never much heeded. Now every one of his sensations acquired an explicit value—and just as earlier it had been immaterial that Alexei Stepanovich Semyonov, this portly and shabbily dressed man who lived in a cheap room, the rent of which, moreover, was in arrears, suffered from rheumatism, so now it was material and significant; and each ailment was attended by its own doctor, masseur and pharmacist, who sold Alexei Stepanovich a multitude of expensive and useless remedies. Previously, Alexei Stepanovich had not been overly concerned with the what and how of his thoughts; now that he had a great deal of free time, however, this leisure began to be filled with constant reflection on many things that appeared before him as though for the very first time.

He looked at the portrait hanging on the wall; it was a portrait of Suslikov's daughter, who had died several years previously. Alexei Stepanovich had known her and remembered all twelve years of her life; he remembered her with a dummy teat in her mouth, then as a young girl in a white frock, and then in Paris when she would come home from school with ink-stained fingers—as had her mother and father and even Alexei Stepanovich himself in their time. Then came a lengthy illness, and Alexei Stepanovich recalled this poor, frail body on top of the bed sheets, tossing and turning, probed by doctors, and her terrible eyes. Whenever he approached her, she would always reach out to him with a pathetic and trusting childish gesture that each time brought tears to his eyes. During the course of her long illness, everyone grew so accustomed to her that almost no one paid any attention to her groaning and quiet sobs; every once in a while her mother, in her brisk, indifferent voice, would utter a few words of tenderness to her, though they were incongruous with those offhand, familiar intonations. Only Alexei Stepanovich, who loved her more than everyone, was unwaveringly attentive to her slightest movement, which caused pain throughout her whole body.

Then, in the last days of her illness, her eyes took on that opaque, leaden hue, which Andrei Stepanovich knew very well and whose significance there was no mistaking. In impotent and mortal despair, while looking into those dimming eyes, Alexei Stepanovich thought that he would give all his life's meagre joy, as well as his life itself, in order to save her; but this willingness of his proved just as worthless as everything else. And soon enough the day came when her eyes were closed, and coins laid over then—and the frail body, after several hours of agonizing death throes, fell still. To Alexei Stepanovich it seemed then that he, too, was essentially dead to everything, and with such stillness and absurd terror all those familiar objects peered at him—the table, the bed, the easy chair—and had lost their former meaning, as had everything in existence. And so Alexei Stepanovich never recovered from this. After witnessing this most terrible sight, whose manifestation had destroyed everything and made senseless and hollow all the good he knew in life, he understood, not with his mind, but with something else infinitely more trustworthy, the terrible and incontrovertible truth, of which it was forbidden to speak and which plunged into an unceasing and fatal sorrow all this vainly existing world. Nothing could aid Alexei Stepanovich in this, and his omnipotent wealth here proved just as inconsequent and superfluous as everything else.

He was left sans desire. Food nauseated him, reading bored him, card games were dull, he had no one to love; and despite the fact that the fates of dozens of people depended indirectly on him, not one of them was interested in his private life. He even had no one to talk to, and he spent increasing periods of time in the easy chair, alone with his wretched feelings. One day he went to Marya Matveyevna, with whom in former days he had felt so happy and at ease; she understood him implicitly, and together they would occupy themselves with what she termed "lyrical journeys". Thus would they discuss everything—happiness, death, wealth, fame, and the only feeling that was possessed of a furious and inexhaustible wealth of thoughts and sensations.

He arrived at her apartment in the afternoon, entered and slumped himself down in an uncomfortable armchair.

"Well, tell me, Alyosha, dear," she said. "Do you recall how you and I would talk back then in Russia and in those first years in Paris?"

"A millennium ago?"

"Yes, a millennium ago. Things were better back then. Tell me, how are you getting on? I hardly ever see you."

And so Marya Matveyevna began to recite. With unmoving eyes, Alexei Stepanovich watched her. He mused that she would begin to talk of the past, of what may yet come to pass, how her life had changed and how now there seemed to be no space in it for those things that had previously been so important. Yet she said none of this. At great length she complained to Alexei Stepanovich about the maid, the soaring prices, and related the protracted tale of why she had been forced to give up the services of Russian dressmakers and turn instead to French ones.

"You see, if you need not even a chic, but just a nice *après-midi* dress—I'm not talking about evening dress—then remember, you need only go to a French dressmaker."

"I have no need of a good dress," said Alexei Stepanovich in astonishment, which pertained to the matter of the dress, and partly to the thought that Marya Matveyevna should speak of such trifles when he had anticipated something quite different.

"No, you misunderstand me."

"Indeed…"

"The point is that they still have ambition, they're all the wives of generals. What does it matter to me that at the close of the nineteenth century one of her husbands commanded some brigade or other? What relation does this fact—pray tell, Alyosha—bear to my present-day dress? How you do stare," she said, suddenly losing her temper, having finally noticed Alexei Stepanovich's steady, piercing gaze.

"You've become somehow more vulgar," he slowly pronounced. "But that isn't the issue: there's something else I want to say to you. Here you are, having lived a rather long life; you had a husband, a lover, children, a daughter who died; you knew years of privation and misery. Can you really now talk to me only of dressmakers and the maid? Is there truly nothing more interesting?"

"No," she replied. "You want to philosophize. No, I've had quite enough of that, I'm not twenty."

"So that's it…"

"So that's it," she repeated. "That's why there are few opportunities and such little time left."

She got up and made for the door, then turned back and with a sharp, quick movement, which was typical of her—and Alexei Stepanovich immediately recognized it, and it reminded him at once of a great many tender and ostensibly forgotten things—placed her hands on his shoulders and sat on his knee; his legs immediately began to ache under the weight of her body. She said nothing and only looked for a moment into his eyes; and he understood in this slightly frightened and repentant look more than she could have said. He understood that in her life everything had been almost as hopeless as in his—with the difference that she still wanted to live and attached a value to certain things that provoked only sadness and disgust in him, and that the matter of dressmakers and the maid interested her only because it stopped her pondering what she ought not to ponder, lest she cry or become upset. But this gaze of hers returned, only for as long it lasted, the possibility of an equal understanding of things, made of her for this moment a fellow traveller of Alexei Stepanovich's in his sorrowful, final journey. But then, heavily and clumsily, she slid off his knee; her skirt hitched up, baring her ample legs, the mere sight of which in former times would have been enough to rob Alexei Stepanovich of several hours' sleep, and which he now regarded as he would any other object—with a dash, perhaps, of a certain, almost imperceptible regret, in which it was possible to discern, under very close scrutiny, traces of a long-extinguished and impotent desire. Immediately thereafter, once she had left the room, he sensed that she would not return to those things that for an instant had come to life in her accidental gaze and disappeared, this time for good.

*

He believed in nothing. Once Anatoly, while showing him a Russian newspaper that had recently come into existence and was foredoomed to a swift closure because of insufficient capital, was talking about an article condemning the Revolution, which had been composed in energetic and the most uncompromising language. "You know, Uncle," he said, "so long as there are people like this in the world…" "Like what?" "Well, convinced…" "Do you want me to prove to you that you're a fool?" "How will you do that?" "Wait and see." This entertained him for a certain time; he telephoned, arranged meetings, discussed things, and a week later, when Anatoly came to visit, he showed him the typescript of an article. Anatoly read it through. The article was consecrated to giving proof that without revolution and revolt, creativity, art, "proud and free thought", and even the prospect of a different, better humanity, were impossible. The article was signed with that same name, so familiar to Anatoly.

"What's all this?" said Anatoly.

"Dear Tolya, it's very simple. It cost me"—he extracted a notebook—"seven hundred and forty-six francs all told."

"How did you do it?"

"Curiosity killed the cat…"

Alexei Stepanovich did not tell Anatoly that he had rung up the author of the article, arranged a meeting, then over lunch in a restaurant said that he was planning to publish a leftist newspaper and that among the regular contributors he, naturally… He said that he was collating material for the first issue, which promised to be a particular success, and would pay a fee up front, at an inflated rate for this issue, and after several days he received the article about art and revolution.

He admittedly knew in advance that everything would be just as he had envisaged, but nevertheless he had not imagined that it would be so easy and inexpensive. And if before the days of his wealth he had not much liked people in general and mistrusted them, then now they incited in him disgust and repugnance. He had always known theoretically that money changes human relationships; yet this had been an abstract knowledge, from which it was possible to draw abstract conclusions about the value of such relationships in general, but which he would discuss as one would any psychological problem. Now he possessed a long experience that was impossible to contradict. He even knew that if Marya Matveyevna were not certain that he would never refuse her—she had merited this through long years of self-sacrifice—she would be just as kind to him as the rest and would not allow herself any sharp rejoinders, though her emotions would not have corresponded to her actions.

Yet she might have allowed herself everything; for too long she had shared with Alexei Stepanovich her frugal dinners, her paltry sums of money, with which they sometimes took themselves to a cheap cinema, shared with him her few joys and her body—all that she had. Alexei Stepanovich was amazed to notice that he felt no gratitude towards her whatsoever and that he was even essentially indifferent to her fate, though he knew that he ought to be grateful and that he ought to do everything he could for her—and, indeed, this he did with cool, indifferent readiness.

Contemplating and recalling all this for the hundredth time, he sought, as he always did, the solution to these questions, the possibility of some escape. But there was no escape. What he had known before, long ago—the turbulent joy of physical existence—had now disappeared, and all his life's current sensations were but an unceasing succession of pain, malaise and a peculiar physical disgust, which he had hitherto not known. From time to time, when people, wishing to receive from him a subsidy for the publication of a radical newspaper, would talk to him of social reform, and when he reflected on the necessity of these reforms, he would reply to them that he had but one life—and a wretched one at that—that he had more important things to think about than other people and that even if he were to abandon all this, no social reforms would change anything; that, at best, come even revolution, there would be a redistribution of wealth and yesterday's proprietors would land in the position of the proletariat; but neither the proletariat nor the bourgeoisie would benefit or become happier from this. The principal changes would be so insignificant that it was not worth undertaking anything for their sake: the publication of a radical newspaper less so than anything else.

After such conversations, however, he would notice that the semi-unconscious conception of the world that he had previously possessed and that consisted in an almost inexhaustible wealth of images that unfolded as he contemplated various things had now become scant and impoverished; nothing remained, bar a dozen pessimistic convictions, a large quantity of physically morbid sensations and something very akin to a never-ending pyrosis of the soul. In vain would he convince himself that the world could not be like this, that there was love, self-sacrifice and the inconceivable beauty of sights and sounds; yet all this was inaccessible to his senses and, consequently, did not exist.

It was then that he realized all the unbearable horror of his life.

*

He took his meal alone in the enormous dining room, flooded with light, at a table around which twenty people could be seated; he ate several morsels of fish, which gave off some tangy and unfamiliar smell, three spoonfuls of very hot soup, a little meat, from which the reddish juice of anaemic blood unappetizingly trickled out unappetizingly, and a mandarin. Coffee and tea were forbidden him.

He rose from the table and retired to his study. The rooms were vast, bright and desolate. Silence reigned in the apartment. The thought flashed through his mind that here he was, an elderly man, unneeded by anyone, living alone in a grand apartment, while thousands of people in that same city slept in the streets and under the bridges. Yet the thought was familiar to him and had long since lost its sentimental association, and for that reason represented the purest abstraction.

Passing through the rooms, he flicked the light switches, turning off the electricity everywhere; and after a while everything was bathed in a deceptive light coming from the street lamps. There was absolute silence. Alexei Stepanovich slowly walked back, from his study into the dining room, in a deathly ennui that seemed inseparable from this pale light, silence and desolation.

He switched on the wireless and heard a voice announcing that a transmission of a Toscanini concert from the Opéra was about to begin. He sat down in the easy chair, closed his eyes and imperceptibly dozed off; when he awoke, the room was filled with sounds, amid the unforgettable movement of which he immediately recognized the *Pastoral* Symphony nearing its end. Then the speaker's voice announced the *Danse macabre*. Alexei Stepanovich winced and switched off the apparatus; but he regretted it and switched it back on. The piece was all too familiar to him and he did not care for it. He began listening and with incredulity and amazement noted that in Toscanini's interpretation it sounded totally different, revealing to him things that he had never before known and that now, listening to the *Danse macabre* for the hundredth time, he understood and perceived anew. When the applause broke out, he hurriedly turned off the radio and, staring fixedly in front of him, thought of Toscanini's futile genius, the wondrousness of which he now understood just as abstractly and impartially as everything else—and, as with everything else, it was powerless to animate even the slightest part of his soul.

He again took to wandering about the apartment. From far away, in the street, the occasional sound of automobile horns came to him, as though from the sea. He contemplated this, then with somewhat brightened eyes rang twice. A moment later there was a knock on the study door.

"Prepare the car," said Alexei Stepanovich. "I'm leaving for Le Havre in a quarter of an hour."

The night was cold and dry. Lying in the quiet vehicle and watching the immobile—as though atop a statue—cap of the chauffeur behind the wheel, Alexei Stepanovich was transported between dream and waking.

Only at dawn, led by the boy in the hotel to a very well-heated room, did he lie down in bed with disagreeably cold sheets and, awaking every half-hour, lay there until midday; then he went out onto the embankment, watched the tall, cold waves for around half an hour, listened to the hissing of their foam and the noise vanishing amid the water's infinite surface, froze through, returned to the hotel, summoned the chauffeur again and was back in Paris by evening, in his apartment, where everything had remained just as unalterable, bright and utterly hopeless.

The following morning Anatoly told him that he had received an invitation to go to England for three weeks and that, if his uncle had no objections…

"What objection could I possibly have?" said Alexei Stepanovich. "Go wherever your heart desires. Do you need money?"

Anatoly declined the money. In this respect he was unlike other people, who ordinarily would never have dreamt of declining it. He spent little and, unlike his mother, who could not do without a thousand and one things whose purpose she did not even know several years previously, but which now were absolutely necessary to her—was very undemanding.

"For the duration of my absence I shall send you a friend of mine, who will stand in for me," said Anatoly. "It's all been arranged. Please, don't worry about a thing, I'm taking the financial burden upon myself and this, too, has been settled."

"Whatever are you saying, Anatoly Alexandrovich?" said Alexei Stepanovich quizzically and politely. "You mean to take the cost upon yourself? You think you must come to my rescue to help me overcome financial strains? Have you been so rich for long? Perhaps you could make me an offer of credit?"

"No, I beg of you…"

"The devil take you," said Alexei Stepanovich. "Allow me to see to my own affairs. When do you leave?"

Anatoly left the following day, and that very morning his proxy arrived. He was a man of around twenty-three or twenty-four, of average height, well and solidly built, and judging by the suppleness and legerity of his movements, which Alexei Stepanovich followed with an involuntary and unconscious envy, it was evident that he was very strong and healthy. His large—womanlike—dark-blue, hungry eyes with deep circles under them did not tally with this appearance and his slicked-back fair hair. In those first moments Alexei Stepanovich wondered whether he was not a drug addict. But afterwards he rejected this theory—the young man's movements were all much too assured and accurate; everything about him indicated an ideal physical equipoise. "But why these idiotic eyes?" Alexei Stepanovich asked himself. "As though they result from some unsatisfied desire."

Before long Alexei Stepanovich became convinced that his temporary secretary was sufficiently well educated and intelligent and possessed a quick mind. However, as he looked at those eyes, he could never quite rid himself of the impression that he was dealing with a man whose whole life was an effort to control himself—an effort, each time crowned with success, like a difficult and dangerous circus act. It happened that several times he caught himself thinking that he was experiencing something akin to physical unease, of the sort that he would feel when watching an acrobat very nearly falling from a trapeze hanging in a high-up and sinister void.

A few days later, however, Alexei Stepanovich learnt the reason for this strange look about the young man, whom, from the very first day of their acquaintance, he had dubbed privately the Acrobat. He invited him to dine with him. After the repast, the Acrobat told Alexei Stepanovich that the principal and sole misfortune in his life was an absence of money.

"Money as a means, of course?"

"Yes, money as a means."

"A means to what?"

"There's a woman I love…"

"*Plus ça change, plus ça reste la même chose*,"* said Alexei Stepanovich with a sigh. The Acrobat said that the woman he loved could not belong to him because he was too poor and had no right to condemn her to an impoverished existence—in a small apartment, without a maid, with cooking and domestic cares, and so forth. According to the Acrobat, this woman was uncommonly beautiful and uncommonly clever.

"Naturally, naturally," said Alexei Stepanovich.

"You doubt it?"

"No, I've just never seen such things in my own life, although I admit they may well exist. But if I follow you correctly, then if you were rich she would live with you?"

"I believe so."

"And you would like to be rich?"

"Yes."

---

* "Nothing ever changes."

Alexei Stepanovich said nothing. He wanted to ask how much she had demanded, but did not, for fear of offending the Acrobat and having thought, moreover, that it would have been much too conventional.

"But she loves you?"

"I believe so, yes."

"And you're certain that if you had the money everything would be fine?"

"It seems that way."

"And you wouldn't want for anything?"

"No. On that point I'm absolutely sure."

Three days later, after luncheon, Alexei Stepanovich said to the Acrobat:

"Just once I'd like to play the role of the fairy-tale magician."

The Acrobat's dark-blue eyes watched him intently.

"I'm glad that I am able to do this for you, although, truth to tell, it isn't all that estimable, since it doesn't cost me much. But I'm old and unhappy. And if my money can at least make someone happy, that's a very good thing. I have every cause to doubt this," he said. "In my experience, money can lessen suffering, but it cannot create what is not there. It has no creative power. But that is the philosophy of an old sceptic, which has nothing to do with you. I shall be happy if this conviction of mine proves false. Go now."

And when the Acrobat, who was at such a loss that he did not even bother to thank him, had already half-closed the door behind him, he shouted:

"Telephone tomorrow, at ten o'clock, I'll give you all the instructions!"

With a clatter he tossed from the table a box of matches, which landed in his line of sight, and he fell to thinking that wealth had no creative power, that the Acrobat was wrong; yet if one supposed for an instant that a miracle were possible, then that was at least one consolation. Now this last resort had been set in motion; and if it turned out to be just as deceitful and ineffective as everything else, then there would remain only… He shrugged his shoulders, stood up and began to pace about the room. Poor Acrobat! He thinks that now, within this perhaps truly splendid body, within his muscles and his chest, will begin that responsive movement that alone is able to make him happy and only now can materialize and expand; and all this was made possible by that same wealth that had been so powerless in Alexei Stepanovich's hands and which was now to acquire a magical authority. "But that authority is illusory," said Alexei Stepanovich aloud, forcefully.

Anatoly returned from London, the Acrobat vanished entirely without trace, and Alexei Stepanovich's life continued along much the same lines as before. Winter passed, the air became warmer; on moonlit nights Alexei Stepanovich would gaze out of the window onto the rows of blossoming chestnut trees. According to Anatoly, the Acrobat was travelling either in Italy or else in South America; the days grew longer and longer. Alexei Stepanovich continued to receive treatment, lived in the same solitude and ceased even to think about many things, for whenever one of those questions that seemed most important to him arose, a rebuttal was to hand even prior to its consideration, as if it were clear a priori and in perpetuity that there could be no mistake and that everything had been judged and sentenced to a premature disappearance with the same certainty that several days would pass and nothing would remain of the milky-white, ethereal river of chestnut blossoms. "But next summer there will be others," Alexei Stepanovich replied to himself and immediately repeated: "Others. These ones, however, will be gone."

Then he would enter into another plane of contemplation and convince himself that he had no time for blossoming chestnut trees and that they could not in the slightest degree have any bearing on his life and could not alter anything within him—neither for the better, nor for the worse.

Later on, he departed for the sea; in the afternoon he felt exhausted from the heat and drank some iced water; in the evening, leaning on his walking stick, he descended to the empty, remote shore to watch the waves. "This would be a good spot to die," he had once thought. It was evening; at dusk there had been a brief spell of rain. The air had grown fresher, smelling more powerfully of the sea. He returned home. Slowly he approached the villa where he was staying, glanced at its dark, open windows, entered, flicked the light switch and suddenly, as though in a distant dream, saw Acrobat's glaring blue eyes and the black muzzle of a revolver aimed at his chest.

THE MISTAKE

(1938)

Vasily vasilyevich had been wandering about the apartment for a whole hour, peering under tables and divans, turning on the lights everywhere—a lazy dusk had already fallen over the city—yet all his investigations had proved fruitless. He had made several tours of all the rooms, rummaging around in the divans and armchairs and poking his hand into their plush recesses, all dust and velvet, where he found scraps of paper, safety pins and the king of spades, which had fallen out of a deck of cards; what he was looking for, however, was nowhere to be seen. Undismayed, he once again set about his explorations; he was about to climb up onto the sideboard, having repositioned the armchair next to it, when suddenly he espied the black corner of his copybook poking out from under a milk-white vase standing on a small end table. He pulled the book towards him. The table shook, but the book remained firmly in place. He gave a sharp tug and then, comically toppling over, both the table and the vase came toppling down, the latter loudly hitting the parquet and shattering into little white pieces that scattered across the floor. Vasily Vasilyevich froze, breath held, listening to the silence, which was all the more surprising after such a resounding crash. It was almost completely dark; the navy-blue divan seemed black, the clock face showed a hazy yellow and the disc of the tail-like pendulum glinted dimly; on the other side of the window—still, like in a painting—were dark trees. Then, a few seconds later, the street lamps lit up and their pale radiance permeated the apartment, illuminating the table on the floor, the milky shards of glass and Vasily Vasilyevich himself, the newly uncovered copybook finally in his grasp. Vasily Vasilyevich was dressed in long breeches and a sailor's jacket. He stood there as though bewitched, his big, deep-blue eyes wide open, staring at the white, motionless debris on the floor. A long time seemed to pass before the unhurried approach of footsteps could be heard, the light came on, and a voice from the doorway said:

"What have you broken, Vasily Vasilyevich?"

Only then did Vasily Vasilyevich begin to cry, covering his face and understanding the irreparability of what he had done.

"Why ever did you touch it?"

Sobbing and incoherent with despair, Vasily Vasilyevich tried to explain that he had been searching for his copybook, that his father that morning had drawn in it a wonderful little demon for him, that the book had been under the vase, that he had tugged at it, and then the vase had accidentally fallen.

"It's all right," said his mother. "Now help me to clear up the shards. Just be careful not to cut yourself."

"Are they sharp?" asked Vasily Vasilyevich.

"Very sharp."

"But the vase wasn't sharp."

"But Vasily Vasilyevich was a very silly boy."

"Was not," said Vasily Vasilyevich.

At first there was just an armchair with a firm, well-sprung seat; then flashed a face of a cinematic beauty; next came a memory of the taste of the water in the bathhouse and the marinated fish that Natasha had prepared the previous day; then two lines from an old letter she had received: *My faith in you knows no bounds, and I hope that while I live there may be nothing to shake this belief.* Now, these lines related to something that mustn't be thought about, something that had effectively ceased to exist. Thought was to be devoted now to other things, to Italian exhibitions, to art and sculpture; however, none of those wielded its usual persuasiveness or weight any longer. And while they did not quite vanish, still, they failed wholly to engulf the attention; they became tiresome and meaningless, like the classroom exercises of yesteryear. The effort required to avoid thinking about something that has very nearly ceased to exist was akin to a physical strain reaching its limit, when the muscles ache and there is a pounding at the temples, and you want to give it all up and end it. In any case, it was unnecessary and to no avail, for life until then had been joyful, successful and proper, just like a classical schema of some abstract theory, flawless in its execution. Life had been composed—till very recently—of a great succession of sensations, memories and concerns, each of which had been a continuation of that same happy principal that was now lost in time and located somewhere far off in the past, perhaps in childhood, on the seashore. Those beginnings had grown richer, more complex, more profound—with time—and more (it seemed) certain; beyond them was just an insignificant external world, almost unreal and powerless over what constituted the very essence of life. But around eight years prior to this, a spectre of doubt had surfaced and then vanished, a stray feeling of inexplicable emptiness, as if, despite all this, something was still missing—but then Vasily Vasilyevich came along, and there could no longer be any misgivings that everything had been settled once and for all in the best and most agreeable manner possible. The days and weeks during this time were especially memorable, and they were characterized by a powerful new awareness of everything that was going on—right down to the smallest, most insignificant detail—and a recognition of the almost limitless profusion of opportunities to have as many experiences and emotions as possible. And as all this came to an end, the resulting state of happiness seemed unalterable, as did everything now in this apartment, where silence and twilight reigned. It was indeed very quiet and dark, and still; everything, it seemed, had already reverted to that classical schema, enriched by yet another day, yet another effort of imagination amid the silence—when suddenly, sharply and unexpectedly, with a desperate, almighty reverberation, the crash of broken glass tore through the apartment.

Vasily Vasilyevich had been asleep for some time, his mouth half open and his head resting on his little arm; Natasha was long gone; the armchair had traded places with the divan, at the head of which now shone a lamp with a green shade; the shards of glass had been cleared away; everything else had been dealt with, but there was still the matter of finding, among all those charming everyday objects that constituted life itself, the blind spot, the *point de départ*, beyond which things sometimes took on new meanings, shedding their former aspect. Where, when and why could this have happened? In the early years there had been cruel intentions, a couple of stolen kisses, but these could be put down to youth, not to depravity or to a lack of understanding right and wrong. Then came love and marriage, the cold stare of a mother who hated all the happy people on this earth, and a blessing from an icon as old as time, so darkened with age that it was impossible to make out the saint depicted on it; the barely distinguishable face, along with its small stern eyes, had turned black, and the nimbus around the head was yellowing, yet all this bore an arbitrary, symbolic meaning, and no one—neither those who gave nor those who received the blessing—so much as looked at the icon, which was returned to its resting place at the end of the ritual, its dried-out verdure, now brown with age, covered over. Still before that, there had been Russia, a bright apartment with enormous windows, school, lessons in foreign languages… "Like all people," scornfully said her mother, who had spent her whole life in expectation of some terrible personal tragedy or some catastrophe, and who considered her comfortable existence degrading and unworthy. She was forever planning to join a monastery or a revolutionary group and would tell her husband that to go on living as they did was shameful and that it had to stop; but she entered no monastery nor any revolutionary group, and she continued attending the theatre and receiving visitors, all the while deeply resenting this life of privilege. She came alive only when misfortune truly befell someone, when a person was at death's door; then, casting all else aside, she would set off in their direction, urging the driver on, summoning doctors, spending untold sums of money, looking after the children and generally doing a great deal of good. These deeds, however, had to be preceded by death, or at least something so severe that no amount of money or any degree of care could ever hope to cure. She did not love her daughter, or her son, or her husband; but then a constant stream of people from all walks of life would come to her—petitioners, wretched-looking individuals, cripples with their eyelids upturned, drunkards, consumptives, unfortunate and pitiful people, to whom she would give money and clothing and for whom she cared as though they were family. Later, as she entered the dining room, whereupon everyone would fall silent, she would say:

"Thanks be to God that we can eat well today."

Her husband would merely shrug his shoulders, having accustomed himself to this daily comedy over the course of thirty years.

She hated, indeed despised, everything that exhibited health, happiness, wealth and love; anything favourable would elicit from her no more than a sneer and hostility. When her daughter's future husband had approached her—this was already abroad, in Berlin, although practically nothing in the house had changed (the same poor wretches would crowd the dark stairwell as before, the only difference being that Germans had started appearing alongside the Russians)—to seek permission to ask for Yekaterina Maximovna's hand in marriage, she had just stood there, silent, staring at him wrathfully, until finally she replied that she was very happy for them; it rang with such hatred and malice that he left, perplexed and almost frightened by this inexplicable ire. On the day of the wedding, wearing a tight-fitting starched dress, she received messages of congratulation and then summoned her daughter to inform her of certain laws of nature, the reproductive instinct, the *plaisirs de la lune de miel*,* and that, when all is said and done, what will have taken place, though distressing, is perfectly normal. She advised her

---

* Pleasures of the honeymoon.

daughter to bear in mind the fact that there were tens of thousands of people starving in Berlin.

Only her father would occasionally say to her:

"There's nothing to be done, Katya. Your mother isn't a happy woman."

It was so astonishing, then, that later, while living in Paris, Katya received her first letter from her mother:

My dear Katya, my darling daughter... It was composed entirely of such tender phrases, never before employed by her; everything was so congenial and warm, so inexplicable and unexpected, that Katya wept as she read the letter and then showed it to her husband, who said that he had always held a higher opinion of his *belle-mère* than others around her, because there was undoubtedly much good in this woman and her actions had just been misinterpreted. On the day that Vasily Vasilyevich was born, the first face Katya saw was her mother's; she, however, left immediately, having ascertained—"with sorrow", as Katya's brother put it—that, regrettably, both mother and baby were well and out of harm's way. When, in the clinic, Katya's mother ran into her own son, whom she had not seen in a number of years, she said to him, "Hello," in an almost enquiring tone. "And what exactly are you doing here?"

"My sister is giving birth, Mother," he replied.

"Precisely. You have absolutely no cause to be here,"

she said, and sailed into the ward from which the screams of her daughter could be heard.

Later, as soon as Katya had recovered, the three of them—Katya, her husband and her brother—celebrated the birth of Vasily Vasilyevich: there was champagne, they sent telegrams to their relatives, they drank toasts to Vasily Vasilyevich, who was peacefully asleep at the other end of the apartment, snugly wrapped up in swaddling clothes. It was Katya's brother, Alexander, who had first called him Vasily Vasilyevich, saying to her:

"Just look how commanding he is. It wouldn't do to call him by his first name alone. He's got to be called Vasily Vasilyevich." Thus it became customary to call him by his first name and patronymic, and everyone later would say in all earnestness:

"Where's Vasily Vasilyevich? What's Vasily Vasilyevich up to?"

Vasily Vasilyevich was a small and chubby baby. First he crawled, then he started to walk around the apartment; he would fall over and, without saying a word, look at everyone with those serious, dazzling eyes. He loved his uncle above all others, then his mother, and then "maybe" his father—as he once said when he was asked this for the hundredth time and first used the word "maybe".

*

THE MISTAKE

She was taking a bath late one evening, before lying down to sleep, when her husband came in. He pushed open the glass door, entered and saw Katya in the bathtub; she suddenly became terribly embarrassed by her body—overwhelmed by a sense of burning, inexplicable shame. Something had changed, something was not quite right. He said, "Forgive me, Katya, *je suis un peu dans la lune*,"* and walked out of the bathroom. The colour rushing to her face, she donned her bathrobe and went through to her bedroom.

He appeared a few minutes later, carrying a cup of tea on a tray. "I thought you'd care for some tea after your bath."

"Thank you. You're a darling, as always."

He sat down on the armchair and told her about the gala dinner he had just returned from; she listened to him with a feeling of detached wonderment, as though noticing for the first time how cleverly he talked about people, how he immediately grasped what was important and what was not, and how he always knew what needed to be said and done. Never yet, it seemed, had he been mistaken—either in his thoughts or in his actions; thus had it ever been, and so she had grown used to

---

* "My head is a little in the clouds."

trusting him implicitly in all matters. She had doubts at first: she tested his instincts, subjected him to a huge variety of experiments, all of which confirmed only the most favourable of hypotheses—whether because he loved her more than anything in the world, as he claimed, or because he was aided by his monstrous, as she thought, intellect. A second theory had developed because the man was, or at least made himself out to be, blind in only one respect—his wife. He trusted nothing and nobody—people, ideas, relationships—and based everything on calculation. Katya was sometimes astonished by his callous estimations of people, although they were almost always proved right; he knew exactly how to talk to different sorts of people and never expressed any superfluous sentiments. He understood everything at once, and only when he was alone with Katya would he let down his guard and be transformed into as helpless a creature as little Vasily Vasilyevich, for he was certain that Katya could never be capable of any misdeed. He bid her goodnight and left the room; she again fell to thinking how it could be possible that this man truly believed her incapable of any wrongdoing. Naturally, he could not account for Katya's having sudden doubts about matters that had been put to bed long ago. Kissing her hand and gazing into her eyes, he understood that he should leave, that she was in no mood for it today. Could it have been that he was just tired? No, she had sensed when he took her hand that this was not the case, and it was only after their eyes had met and his fingers had slowly and affectionately let go that he smiled, kissed her hand and silently made his exit.

His infallibility began to unnerve her sometimes—as if he were not a man, but a perfect, thinking machine. It seemed to require from him no effort whatsoever to know what would please her and what she would find disagreeable, even down to the slightest remark about a dress she was wearing for the first time. She would occasionally start to make cutting, unjust remarks, but he always kept calm and just smiled, and in his smile there was not even a shadow of derision—she would never have forgiven him for that—but only tenderness. He would smile at Vasily Vasilyevich much in the same way. It was thus that he made a complete study of Katya—her hidden desires, her unprompted, ill-reasoned ideas, all her variations. He studied her as easily as he would any problem he was addressing and was able to develop an exact formula, like an algebraic equation.

Yes, and until lately he had been right about everything. But one day, when Katya asked him what it took to know a person inside out, he replied:

"A lover's intuition."

"What about the people you don't love? The general order of things?"

"I don't think there is a general order of things."

"Then what is there?"

"The fact that every man projects a personality that can be likened to another's by casual analogy; although, this is governed not by its own set of rules, of course, but by various associations, characteristic of a certain point in time…"

"Lord, how complicated it all is! But is it actually possible to know a man through and through?"

"No, of course not. One could predict how he might act in a narrow set of circumstances, but even that would be far from certain."

"But you're so rarely mistaken."

"Oh, I make mistakes all the time," he said, smiling. "It's just that mistakes are seldom irreparable, and I try not to repeat them."

"What about me?"

"I know you intuitively, unthinkingly, because I love you."

It was after one o'clock in the morning, but she was still awake, searching, trying to understand when and how this mistake had occurred. Up to a point, it had all been clear: her life, she thought, as she lay on her back in the dark, was being played out on two stages—one on top of the other. On the first was her husband, whom she loved, Vasily Vasilyevich, her father and brother—bringing her joy to varying degrees and in different ways. The other, to which she almost never gave any thought, but which was self-evident and as distinct as the first, consisted in a sound knowledge of a number of theoretical stances: this knowledge would allow one, for example, to discern accurately whether an act was right or wrong. In the world there was disease, death, misery, hatred, resentment, deceit and betrayal, but none of this could touch her or her loved ones. These things were known to everyone, yet to her they were abstract concepts, knowledge that had never been tested, like the image of a country she had never visited. It did not occur to her that she might one day experience something in this vein. And so a change took place in this network of thoughts and feelings. Where yesterday there had been a dark, empty space, something new and repugnant—in terms of these former notions—now emerged; moreover, it had been deliberate and was nearly as vast in scope as everything that had existed for her until now—a whole new world unlike anything she had experienced before, dangerous, dark and overwhelming.

It was simple enough to establish the facts. First an evening with her husband at the theatre, then an acquaintance—a young man around five years her senior, of uncertain nationality, with a decent command of Russian, of fairly athletic build, and in no way exceptional on first appearance. For some reason he irritated her, although there seemed to be nothing to find fault with. Later he paid them a visit—a first, then a second the following week.

"Do you have much free time?" she asked.

"My whole life," he replied, smiling. "I recently came into an inheritance."

Then came the first time they stepped out together, a matinee show at the cinema, a taxi, his approaching lips and the unbearable desire to grip that mouth with her teeth—and the morning after, the pale winter's light in the window and her own naked body emerging from the bed sheets.

She went home. Her husband had gone out, and Vasily Vasilyevich was building a tower out of iron strips. Ten minutes later the telephone rang, and her husband's voice informed her that he would not dine at home, that it would be too late by the time he returned.

"Fine," she answered.

She and Vasily Vasilyevich ate together. Later her brother arrived with some amusing anecdotes and stayed until one o'clock in the morning. Gradually the deathly melancholy that had accompanied her journey home vanished, as though seeping lazily into the distant gloom; then, lifting up her bright eyes, Katya began to feel as though she was back to her usual self, that everything was in its rightful place—and that she loved everything she had previously loved just as much as before.

Three days passed. The telephone rang, and in a strange, altered, drained voice she said that, fine, she was willing—then came a repeat of the first time: first the lips and a buzzing throughout her whole body, then the slow fingers at her breast and legs, and finally that last, indescribably drawn-out motion, the glistening beads of sweat on both face and body, and the touch of firm, burning skin—the realization that she was suffocating and that it could be the most wonderful death.

After that, it became a regular occurrence. It had not the slightest bit to do with love or affection, and it was purely by chance that the young man turned out to be an impeccable, kind and decent fellow in his relations with Katya; moreover, their assignations were surrounded by such secrecy that no one apart from them knew about it. If Katya did not meet him during the course of the week, she would begin once more to feel as though nothing had happened; but all it took for her was the sound of his voice, and she would be prepared to travel anywhere; she was utterly incapable of fighting this urge. They never left a place together and were careful never to be seen in each other's company. He stopped visiting Katya's apartment altogether, and her brother, Alexander, even asked one day:

"Whatever happened to that alcoholic, Katya?"

"What alcoholic?"

"Oh, you remember, that young chap, dark-haired, I seem to recall—the rich heir."

"Yes, I remember. Only why do you call him an alcoholic? Do you know him well?"

"I don't know him from Adam. But I don't have to. Just look at him—always pristine, well dressed, cheery… That, my dear, is suspicious. Eventually it'll all come out: he's an alcoholic."

"You're such an idiot, Sasha."

"Well, I'm telling you that you don't know the first thing about psychology. My eyes never fail me. It's a crime that I'm an architect: I should have been a scientist."

"Oh, it certainly is a crime that you're an architect."

It was with some astonishment that Katya observed how seldom she spoke with her lover and that conversation with him was entirely unnecessary. Right from the very start, however, she had begun to feel, in tandem with this irresistible attraction to him, something verging on hatred.

THE MISTAKE

He could not fail to notice this and even said to her one day that perhaps it would be better if they put an end to their trysts—if she did not love him…

"I've never loved you," she said. "Never, do you hear? Never. But I cannot live without you."

"That is far too complicated for me."

"Yes," she said, with regret and contempt. "That's true. It *is* too complicated for you."

She was beginning to rot inside; she would fly into a rage for no good reason and, one day, in the presence of her brother and her husband, she slapped Vasily Vasilyevich right in the face—the boy was so stunned by the act that he did not even cry. Her brother shot up and shouted so loudly that his voice filled the entire apartment:

"You stupid woman!"

She looked at him, and then at her husband—for the first time she noticed his cold, foreign eyes. Without raising his voice, he said:

"Thus far I have not taken advantage of my rights, Katya. Now, however, I am compelled to do so. There are things that I cannot and will not allow."

"The older you get, the more you're like Mother," said Alexander furiously. "A pretty inheritance."

"I don't think that's the issue here, Sasha," said her husband measuredly.

It ended in hysterics, tears and Katya's lying down on her bed and not getting up until the following morning.

She became perfectly insufferable. She would scold the maid constantly, fuss bitterly, rearrange the furniture in the apartment, demand, refuse, purchase things and send them back; she lost any resemblance to the meek woman she had once been. Her husband went abroad for a month and Vasily Vasilyevich went to his uncle's "for a visit", as his uncle put it, and she was left alone. She thought she was close to suicide. She felt as though she could no longer endure such a life.

Then one day he did not show up for their assignation. She sat a whole hour in the little apartment he rented for their meetings, but he did not come. She left. She waited for the telephone to ring or for a note, thinking that some catastrophe might have befallen him. But there was no call, nor any note.

A week passed. She spent it reading books that she was unable to understand, no matter how hard she tried. She began writing letters to her husband, only to throw them away, unfinished, and await an explanation, despite outward appearances, for what had happened.

Late one evening, a week and a half to the day since their failed assignation, an unfamiliar voice informed her over the telephone that Monsieur So-and-So was very keen to see her. She brusquely hung up, but a minute later the same voice called again and explained that she had misunderstood, that she was mistaken—*monsieur* was in a very bad way and that if she did not come immediately…

"I'm coming," she said. "The address, please."

Ten minutes later she entered his unfamiliar apartment. A doctor's assistant with a very grave expression—one that people have only in exceptional and usually dire circumstances—had opened the door to her, and from this she knew that he must be dying. The doctor, with a hardened, absent-minded expression on his unshaven face, walked past her, seeming not to notice her presence. A few other people had gathered in a large reception room; she knew none of them, but, looking at each one, she was able to read the situation accurately. It was warm and stuffy in the apartment, and a medicinal smell mingled with a strange, foul odour. Through the reception room, towards Katya, came another assistant, carrying a large object under her spotless white apron. A young man sitting in an armchair raised his head, glanced at Katya as one would at a table or a chair, and lowered his head, cradling it in his hands.

No sooner had Katya entered than she was hit by a palpable, chilling, almost unbearable languor. She stood for a moment, crossed herself and finally went into the room where the patient lay. At first sight of him, she felt a strange, insurmountable terror.

He lay on the bed, covered up to his waist. Instead of the torso that she knew so well, with its rippling muscles under dark, firm skin, she saw a tightly covered ribcage with angularly protruding bones. His arms were thin and his fingers too large. She leant over the unfamiliar, overgrown face. His eyes had rolled back into their sockets; in place of the irises were two frozen, jaundiced whites. His mouth lay open. The dying man's breathing was strangely shallow and quick, like a dog's after a run. He was unconscious.

She knelt before the bed and took his burning hand; he gave no sign of feeling this. Then, for a second, his eyes appeared and he looked upon Katya, failed to comprehend what was going on and wheezed in an unfamiliar voice: "Oxy… oxy…"

"He's asking for oxygen," said Katya.

"Yes, yes," came the doctor's absent-minded voice from the reception room, apparently in response to a question from his assistant. "But it's futile all the same, all the same."

Overnight his breathing grew slower and slower, and at four o'clock in the morning, without having regained consciousness, he died. Her cheeks moist, Katya left the room. The young man sitting in the chair, the deceased's brother, was crying inconsolably, sobbing like a child. Only then did it become apparent to Katya, what had long been so, but had never managed to reach her consciousness: namely, that the man who had died was the man she loved, and that she had loved only him.

She returned home, lit a cigarette and sat down to write a letter. At eight o'clock in the morning her husband arrived on the early train. He kissed her hand, looked at her much-altered face and said in French (he often switched to French):

"*Tu reviens de loin.*"*

"*Je ne reviens pas,*" she said. "*Je pars.*"†

That very day, having signed the petition for divorce, she left.

---

* Literally, "You're coming back from afar"; metaphorically, "You've dodged a bullet."
† "I'm not coming back… I'm leaving."

THE BEGGAR

(1962)

High up, on the Elysian Fields, where in these winter months from four o'clock in the afternoon neon advertisements glow and the windows of the enormous cafés are illumined, icy sleet was falling, while down below, in the long subterranean passageways of the Métro, the air was warm and still. In the middle of one of these underpasses, always in exactly the same spot, stood an old man in rags, hatless and with a dirty-pink bald patch, around which, above his temples and above the nape of his neck, grey hairs protruded in all directions. As with the majority of Paris's poor, he was dressed in some shapeless garb. Both his overcoat and his trousers looked as though they had ever been thus, as if they had been made to order like that, with those soft creases, with that absence of any lines or contours, like a dress or a great sackcloth robe that people belonging to another world, and not the one surrounding them, would wear. This man was standing not far from a blind youth who would play the accordion for hours at a time and only ever the same melody—Ravel's *Boléro*—standing between two advertisements: one depicted a grinning, mustachioed man holding a cup of coffee, the brand and quality of which were indicated below, where a clean line severed the man's body and below which it was said that there was no finer coffee. On the second advertisement a young blonde with an ecstatically happy expression on her porcelain-and-pink face was hanging on a clothesline deathly white bed sheets, which had been washed in some warm water to which had been added a special powder, imparting to the laundry a never-before-seen whiteness. The colossal posters bearing these advertisements had hung in that same place for years, just as the old beggar had stood there, never moving, just like the mustachioed gentleman with the cup of coffee and the blonde with her hand—petrified on the paper—reaching towards the bed sheets. Yet he did not see these advertisements; rather, they produced no impression in his optics, and if someone were to have asked him what was depicted upon these sheets of paper, he would not have been able to recall.

However, no one ever asked him anything. For many years, since he had become a beggar, one of the peculiarities of his existence had consisted in the fact that he had

THE BEGGAR

almost ceased speaking, not only because he lacked the urge to do so, but also because there was no necessity. Words and their meaning had long since lost for him their former value, as had everything that preceded his current life. One day he spotted a discarded newspaper: it was lying on the grey floor of the passageway in the Métro, and on the front page, in enormous lettering, were printed the words: "WAR IN KOREA". He looked at the newspaper with his dull eyes and marked neither the combination of letters nor their meaning. This war, which was being followed by millions of people the whole world over, did not exist for him, as nothing else existed, except for his own protracted delirium, through which he was slowly but surely moving towards death. Sometimes, when at night he would leave the Métro and walk through the deserted streets of Paris, across the entire city, towards a wasteland on the periphery, where there was an enormous wooden crate in which he would spend the night, he would be stopped by policemen and asked his name, his place of address and whether he had any money. Without looking at those who asked these questions, he would reply that he was called Gustave Verdier and that he lived near the Porte d'Italie. Then he would extract from his pocket and show them several credit notes, always the same ones. The policemen would let him go, and he would continue on his way. Late at night he would reach his crate, open the batten door, fastened by a hook, crouch, enter and immediately lie down on a mattress that served as his bed. He had acquired this crate after an old man, a beggar like him, who had built it himself and obtained the mattress from somewhere or other, died one summer's night from a heart attack and was found by the police several days later; they discovered his death because it was hot and the body of the old man had begun to decompose. When the crate became free, Gustave Verdier entered it and had remained there ever since. The crate was permeated by the corpse's stench, to which he became accustomed and which gradually altered later, acquiring ever newer nuances. At first the foetid smell in the crate took his breath away; but then it became easier, as if amid this poisoned air some doubtful equilibrium between the danger of suffocating and the ability to breathe had been established. In the crate there remained, from the old man who had died in it, a little mirror of polished steel—everything it reflected took on a cold metallic tint; there was also a candle, a box of sulphur matches, a little water basin, a small pail, a dented razor, a sliver of soap and a grey rag through which the light shone and which served as his towel. All this, which was embedded in that final conception of the world that the old man took with him to the grave, lay on a little cardboard box for tins of food, except for the pail, which stood in the corner. The old man owned nothing else.

All this—the crate with the mattress, the long hours in the subways of the Métro, the slow nocturnal peregrinations across the sleeping city, the fact that the majority of the people he met or who walked past him brazenly avoided him and looked at him with unseeing eyes, as they might have looked at an empty space—all this had appeared to him during the course of the past weeks and months in the most vague and uncertain terms, as though through a shroud of mist. He had long forgotten that it was possible to experience hunger: he had never starved, for there was always money for a piece of bread, cheese and wine; what was more, in the early hours it was easy to find scraps of food in the rubbish bins lining the streets; at the Central Market it was enough merely to traipse through it to fill your bag with vegetables picked up off the ground. Now, however, he needed very little to sate himself. He would go to sleep and awake with that same noise in his head, which had begun recently and which muffled and drowned out all the other sounds that reached him. Sometimes he had the sudden feeling that his chest was being constricted by an iron band: he would begin to suffocate and everything around him would be submerged at once in this feeling of pain and cease to exist. Then he would close his eyes and lean against the wall, nearly losing consciousness. Several minutes later the pain would abate; he would open his eyes again and look ahead of himself hazily, at the grey walls surrounding him, at the people passing him by, at the advertisements he didn't see. He had long since ceased not only to contemplate anything, but also to think altogether; it was the same as the vanished need to speak. In this mute and unthinking life there remained only the interchange of sensations—the noise in his head, pain, fatigue, the itching from insect bites, the heavy stench of the crate that he would detect upon entering it after a long stint in the open air, cold, heat, thirst. Recently something new had been added to all this; it was also a sensation, but a very peculiar, chilling and insistent one. Then, for the first time in all these years, he made a supreme effort over himself (something he was long unaccustomed to doing), thought about this and at once understood both the meaning of the noise in his head and the feeling of the iron band around his chest. He recalled his age—he was seventy-six—and it became apparent to him that his long life was approaching its end and that nothing could now change this. From that day on, standing in the corridor of the Métro, now closing, now opening his eyes, he began anew to think about those things that had occupied his thoughts many years ago. It had been so infinitely long ago, long before he became as he was now. The question, which had so importunately faced him back then and to which, as he knew both then and now, there was and could be no answer, was that as to the meaning of life, why it was necessary, and to what mysterious end this long sequence of events had been set in motion, having now led him here, to this warm brick tunnel under the Elysian Fields. Through the noise in his head he again heard the melody that the blind boy would play on his accordion. Until now he had been so far removed from his surroundings that he had conceived of this music as a mechanical irritation of his audition, without realizing what it was. Now he suddenly recognized this melody and recalled that it was Ravel's *Boléro*, which even in former times he had been unable to abide; it had always seemed to him that this blunt repetition of the same barbaric sounds, their savage and primitive rhythm, contained something that affected the nerves. The *Boléro* provoked in him almost physical revulsion. When had he last heard this? He made an effort and recalled that it had been a long time ago, at a concert. He saw distinctly before him the concert hall, the conductor's tailcoat, his bald head, rows of chairs, a multitude of familiar faces, male and female, which emerged in front of him either in the black and white frames of dinner jackets, collars and ties, or in the anaemic pallor of women's powdered necks and shoulders, terminating where their dresses ended, above the cut lines of which glittered in various shimmering tones their necklaces. He remembered how the conductor jerked convulsively in time to the music and how with those same jerking movements up and down the violins' strings the bows rose and fell. He was sitting in the second row, never turning his head in the direction of his wife, lest he see her face and the cold, inane expression in her eyes. It was an evening in December, with the same icy rain as now, but in the concert hall it had been warmer than in the subways of the Métro. After the concert came a late-night restaurant, white wine and oysters, and in the restaurant he felt just as ill-tempered as he had in the concert hall, and he longingly watched his wife's fat fingers tirelessly work the shells she held, and he looked forward to the time when he would finally return home and be alone with a sense of illusory and short-lived freedom. This return home, to the suburb of Paris where his villa was located, the fact that he would walk into his bedroom and lock the door behind him—this was essentially like his return to that crate where he now lived, with the difference that now he was free.

The blind youth paused for a while, and the *Boléro* faded away. The old man went on thinking, still trying to apprehend something that seemed (to him) so uncommonly important, the chance to explain everything that was slipping away from him. He was free now—because nobody needed him; he had no belongings, no money, no ability to influence anything anywhere, no ability to help or harm anyone in any way, in a word, nothing—nothing that could have tied him to other people and established any obligation between him and them. He even had no name, for there were thousands upon thousands of people who shared his surname, so many that it had become almost anonymous and no one could have supposed that this beggar, with the dirty-pink bald patch enclosed by a trim of grey hair, standing in the corridor of the Métro under the Elysian Fields, and that Verdier who had attended the concert where a performance of Ravel's *Boléro* had been given, and about whose disappearance every newspaper had written all those years ago, could have anything at all in common. As to the reasons for this disappearance, no one had guessed, and not one of the hypotheses set out in those newspaper articles bore the slightest relation to reality—suicide, an irrepressible passion for some unknown woman, a double life that preceded this, financial embarrassment. His finances turned out to be in perfect order, there had been no double life, just as there had been no passion, no unknown woman. People who belonged to the same milieu as Verdier were unable to comprehend how such a man as he could renounce the life he had led and become a vagrant and beggar—unless some imperative reasons had brought him to this—bankruptcy, ruin, insanity, alcoholism.

But there had been nothing of the sort—and so for this reason, in the realm of those ideas that governed all possible actions in this milieu, there was not and could not be any explanation for what had happened. In this milieu there were, however, people of so-called enlightened views, several of whom were writing historical or sociological dissertations on the causes of some revolution or rebellion of immiserated people against their fate and those whom they deemed to blame for it, against the landowning class. Yet none of the authors of these dissertations could admit the possibility of a voluntary rejection of that very same wealth in the name of whose problematic acquisition—according to them—revolutions took place. Just as it was natural to imagine a poor man who strived for prosperity and wealth, so too was it unnatural to conjure up the reverse—that is, a rich man who strove for poverty. Verdier understood this perfectly. From these words—wealth, poverty and rebellion—it was possible to devise different combinations; however, the principal word nevertheless remained "rebellion". Verdier had no aversion to wealth and no lust for poverty or destitution. Yet all his life—until he attained freedom, having renounced what others considered the greatest blessing—he silently and constantly rebelled against that system of oppression that surrounded him on all sides and forced him to live not as he desired, but as he ought to live. Nobody ever asked him whether he wanted this or not. It was immaterial: this question did not exist. What existed was the firm Verdier et fils, which manufactured precise measuring instruments for metallurgical factories. In this firm there were employees and workers, beginning with the director and ending with the janitors. And this firm belonged to Verdier, first to *père*, then to *fils*.

The firm's owner had once had a great many obligations relating to the most varied of people who were connected to him in one way or another. He had a house, a wife, children, a servant, a chauffeur; he made charitable donations and bank transactions; he hosted parties, went to the theatre, concerts, negotiated with deputies in parliament, made connections, attended briefings on the status of his business, on the reorganization of some division or other, had to be at certain places at certain hours, had to respond to some speech, to speak on the evolution of the economy, had to travel hither and thither by train, automobile, ship, aeroplane, stopping in some hotel, had to read some newspaper, had to have an opinion on some composers or artists—thus appeared the system of his perpetual oppression, from which he had long been unable to see any escape. He could, of course, divorce his wife, although in his situation and at his age, and in regard to his children—a mature son, a young engineer who had already begun to grow bald, and a daughter, a plump-cheeked girl with her mother's cold eyes and a piercing voice—this was seemingly not the appropriate course of action. He could divorce, though this would engender a whole host of new complications. Moreover, divorce would not save him from the other obligations, which would remain just as they were. While he received his education, first at the *lycée* and then at university, before, as his father would say, he "truly entered upon life", he hardly suffered from this system of oppression, though even then he would pose himself that same question, to which he was never able to find an answer and which tormented him his entire life: what mysterious and unfathomable combination of millions upon millions of different causes or accidents had determined first his appearance in the world, and later his life; what was the meaning of this and how did it differ from the meaning of other people's existence? And if there were no meaning—which seemed the most likely answer—then what replaced it? A void? On the other hand, if the concept of meaning did not exist, then, it followed, nor did morality. But if morality did not exist either, then there would be what someone had once foretold, that without the threat of retribution, policing and state authority, people would act according to their nature, leaving on earth only ruins, corpses and pregnant women. Yet that suggested that morality was the state and the police—that is, the embodiment of collective policing, the instinct for the self-preservation of society, and so-called individual morality was but fear, heredity and fastidiousness, and in no way the shimmering and perfect reflection of man's meaning and significance on earth. When in his youth he would think about this, it was essentially an abstract problem. And when he finally did "enter upon life", from the very outset this took on a tragic character, in comparison with which everything that had preceded this period seemed idyllic and happy. How could all this have happened? Verdier recalled returning from England, where his father, in his day, had sent him, deeming it necessary that he complete his education namely there, at Oxford.

He was twenty-four years old, and many things interested him—music, painting, literature, philosophy. Least of all did he think of business, for there was no need. He intended to become a writer: he believed that therein lay his vocation, and he forever sought a subject for his first novel—and only then, much later, did he understand that under no circumstances would he ever become a writer—precisely because he was seeking a subject. Unable to find one, he began to ponder the need for something like a treatise on the peculiarities of English prose, but this got no further than a few lines. In the July of the following year, two days after he arrived in the Midi, where he was planning to spend the summer, he received a telegram informing him that his father was gravely ill. When he returned home, he saw only the corpse of his father, who had died the previous evening from an apoplectic seizure. Later came the funeral, eulogies, the reading of the will, and then began that inescapable enslavement, all these eternal obligations and everything that attended them. Several months later he realized that, for as long as it continued, he would never have time for what was called a private life. His mother, whose health was becoming worse and worse, would tell him in a feeble voice that the Verdier family must have an heir, that he must realize that life would not wait for him, that the years would pass by, and so on—in short, that he must marry. So with that same inevitability with which Verdier had attended the funeral of a father, whom by rights he knew only slightly, for when he was a child he would rarely see him, since his father was always busy, and later would see him with even less frequency, since he studied and lived abroad—with this same inevitability he later attended his own wedding; his acquaintance with his future wife was altogether brief, and soon enough he asked himself how all this had happened. Only afterwards did he discover the answer to this, an answer that was for him tragic and unflattering in equal measure. Within her, back then, despite the cold void of her eyes—that same void in which later he would perceive distinctly something else, which without hesitation he defined as stupidity—within her—in her movements, in the contours of her body—there had been some warm, animal allure. That was one answer. A second was that from the very start of their acquaintance she had borne herself with an unshakeable conviction that everything must come about just as it does, and no otherwise, as if everything was clear and set in stone, and since it was inevitable, regardless, Verdier also unwittingly adopted that same tone, and when he suddenly bethought himself that he was planning to do something important, something that he did not at all want to do, it was already too late. Perhaps it had not quite been like that, but thus did it now seem to him, and it struck him that the memory of a seventy-six-year-old man was powerless to reproduce the feelings that he had experienced back then, when he was twenty-five and, essentially, another man. Perhaps it had not been like that, perhaps there really had been some emotion that was now forgotten utterly and irrevocably, and that had been significantly weaker than, for instance, the memory of the taste of oysters after a concert where there had been a performance of Ravel's *Boléro*. Later he had lovers who would submissively undress when he visited them in the evenings. Even then he knew that not one of them truly loved him, and this was understandable: he himself had never experienced an irresistible attraction to a woman, or that feeling of love about which he had so often read in books. Instead of this, there was something akin to physical thirst, tormenting, exhausting, irritating; and when the thirst had been quenched, all that remained was the unpleasant dregs, and nothing else. Later he realized that he was too spiritually impoverished to experience true emotion, and for a certain while this idea was very disagreeable to him. Although he later stopped thinking about it.

He remembered having the reputation of being a very good and generous man, one who helped everyone who appealed to him for aid. However, that, too, was false: he was, essentially, neither good nor generous. He truly did refuse no one, yet he acted thus because he was vexed by those who would tell him in dreary words of their penurious lives, which held no interest for him in the slightest. He always hastened to terminate these conversations and would gladly give whatever sum they asked for. What was more, he genuinely did not begrudge the money, though not because he was generous, but rather because he could never understand how people could attribute to it such a value that it did not have. He needed money only for the sake of other people—his wife, his children, the employees of his firm, others still, but not for himself.

In the distance, around a bend in the long corridor, the last train rumbled past. Verdier removed from his spot, walked slowly up the stairs and exited onto the Elysian Fields. The watery sleet had now stopped, but there was an icy wind. Dragging his feet along the cold slabs of the pavement, he again began his long peregrination across the city, to that spot where, near the Porte d'Italie, the illuminated places ended, and where the wasteland in which his crate stood loomed black. He walked the familiar road, without looking about him, and continued to ponder those things that had seemingly so long ago been buried and forgotten irretrievably, but which now rose up before him once again. When he was around fifty, and when everything he was obliged to do wearied and vexed him, when even the little that had previously given him a certain satisfaction had vanished—a particular note in the taste of the wine at a restaurant, the feeling of the soft bed he would lie in late at night, that beatific state whenever he felt he was about to fall asleep—it was during this time that he began again to read. Until then, over the course of many years, he would read only newspapers. Now he took to books, those same ones that he had read once upon a time at university and whose contents had then so captivated him. Now they had all changed beyond recognition. Rather, it was not what was in these books that had changed. No, it was far more tragic. The more he read various authors, the more he became convinced that he had lost the ability to comprehend the motivations and emotions that compelled the characters of these works to act in one way or another. Why was it necessary to sacrifice everything in one's life for the sake of wealth or power? For money had no value, and power engendered tedious obligation. Why wage war? For every war was senseless. Why did Hamlet have to kill Polonius? Why did people go in for privations and death, especially death, which would come all the same, sooner or later, and which it was pointless to precipitate?

Why spend sleepless nights thinking that your beloved has left you for another, and why try to prevent her, for, even if you were to succeed, her presence would no longer carry any value? Why envy and, more importantly, what to envy? This was the only period in his life when his existence had been shattered by something well and truly tragic—for it was then that he sensed everything was over. He would think about this—back then, all those years ago—from dawn till dusk and could not wait for the moment to come when he would be left alone, late in the evening, in his room. When this moment finally did arrive, he lay down on his bed—and suddenly he realized what it was that separated him from the characters of the books he read and from the people around him. He subconsciously compared himself to a tree, of which the trunk remains but the inside of which is rotten, decayed and dead. It seemed to him that his present existence contained something, as if within its essence he carried his own death. To live meant to have desire, to strive for something, to defend something. He had none of this. And yet, he did retain one desire—freedom. But this, too, was worthless. He did not require freedom to do something that was otherwise prohibited or out of reach. What had seemed to him back then a striving for freedom was simply the renunciation of all the many obligations that rested on him, the renunciation of the world in which he lived and in which he found nothing to justify his presence in it or somehow to atone for it.

He had heard and read many times that people would begin life over again, a sort of second, new life. Yet he lacked the strength for this, and what was more, he simply failed to see to what end, to what purpose it was worth beginning something new—that is, those same exertions and obligations all over again. He recalled—for the thousandth time—those factors that impel people to work or great exploits: conceit, aspiration for riches or power, love for a woman, love for one's country and the desire to benefit it, and, lastly, love for one's neighbour and the desire to help him or to lighten his burden. Of all these, the only one that seemed worthy to him was love for one's neighbour. Yet it was impossible to engender this artificially. On the other hand, it was also impossible to continue the life he was leading, in which among the great many obligations the most onerous was that of lying to everyone around him and to everyone in general whom he met. Lying meant pretending that he was the same sort of man as they were, that he was prepared to play his role to the bitter end. It was not easy for him to take that decision that nobody ever understood. He did not know how his life would subsequently turn out. But he did know that he could no longer remain in the world he had inhabited until then.

So now, crossing Paris at night and heading towards his crate, he thought about all this. He found it difficult to walk; there was a ringing in his ears and his legs ached. Amid the cold, clear air of the winter's night, the lamps appeared to him as hazy, luminous dots. He sat down on a bench and immediately fell asleep. He dreamt that he was walking across a snowy field, through a blizzard, that he felt very cold and that someone's mocking voice was telling him things that, try as he might, he could not understand, while these sounds and words drew nearer and nearer to him and, at the last second, someone demanded that he repeat the words. He made an effort to take himself in hand and eventually repeated them, forgetting them again in an instant. He awoke and then fell asleep once more. Then he awoke for a second time, got up from the bench and walked on, almost blindly, in the direction he knew so well. He sensed his legs failing him, just as if their bones had become soft; he sensed the ground slip away from under them, but still he kept walking, by dint of a terrific and unconscious fiat of will. Whole hours seemed to go by, until at last he arrived at his crate and collapsed onto the mattress.

When he opened his eyes, he saw that daylight was shining in through the chinks in the boards. He got up, sensing in astonishment that his fatigue of the previous night had passed. Having taken a draught of the cloudy water that was left in the pail, he went outside. The day was grey, warmer than on the previous evening. Everything he had thought of came back to him with phenomenal clarity, and the only thing remaining was to draw some definitive conclusions. But this was the most difficult thing of all. Despite appearances, despite that great distance separating him as he was now from the person he had been before, it was clear that all his life—both then and now—still, in spite of it all, retained some meaning and was marked by a definite pattern. In what he had done, having forsaken his house and become a vagrant, chance, about which he often thought, had played no role whatsoever. "Ruins, corpses and pregnant women." No, not only those. Apart from them there would still be people—those like him; those who shared none of the common passions, common aspirations that define human life—that is, those who never dream of becoming a general, a marshal, a bishop, a deputy, a banker, an accountant, a Don Juan, a hero, the bearers of unwanted status, those in whom that pale and dying flame that can be extinguished at any moment barely flickers. Here, in essence, is what ought to be said about him and those like him. He was born poor, with no status—that which his father had left him—nor any circumstances—those in which he had lived for so long—could alter this. If there was anything accidental in his life, it was not what was now, but what had come before it: Verdier et fils.

He reached the entrance to the Métro on the Elysian Fields, descended the staircase, took up his usual place and again heard the *Boléro*. What meaning did his life have? For the first time it was clear to him: he had fulfilled his purpose on earth. Someone's higher will—if one were to grant the existence of such a thing, which, of course, could be considered a hypothesis that was in no way proven, though on the other hand, it was just as impossible to prove otherwise—had determined his fate: to elude temptation and passion and to live out on earth his allotted time, like an animal or a plant, until the moment when this life reached its end. "Blessed are the poor in spirit…" Suddenly he saw before him a painting he remembered. He had seen it in Bonn. It showed the Day of Judgement: from a jagged crevice the naked bodies of people emerged into the light, revealed to their waists, while for others the only thing visible was their hands, which they were using to move away the earth covering their graves.

He stood in his usual spot, in the corridor of the Métro, and silently laughed—for the first time in many years. Did they mean to make a respectable citizen of him, a knight of the Legion of Honour? a captain of industry? perhaps a deputy? perhaps even a minister? Not one of them could fathom such a simple truth, that he had once been so infinitely removed from all this, and that this, in whose name people suffered, performed great deeds and committed crimes or plain villainy—that for him all this had ceased to exist. He belonged to another world. He was unlike those around him, and herein lay the meaning of his life. He had asked no one for this life. He had demanded nothing from anyone—neither from that higher will about which he had begun to think in recent days, nor from other people. Yet the world, such as he ought to accept it, and as did the people around him, who found in it some closure and justice—this world was simultaneously hostile and alien to him. He had always felt that there was no room for him there and that there was nothing for him to do among these people. He had been given life, but in it he found nothing that was worth fighting for or that ought to be resisted, nothing that justified any effort. He was content to exist, for there was no other way, and, what was more, no one ever questioned him about this. Yet to press this existence into those confines in which it should have passed—this he could not and would not do.

Never had everything seemed so clear to him as it did now. And with that same clarity he felt the life slowly departing him. It became difficult to breathe, the outlines of objects lost their definition, the colour of the neon tubes in the Métro tunnel began to look grey. Yet he felt no fear, no pity: there was nothing to fear and, of course, nothing at all to regret. In this slow return to non-being there was even some allure, the delight of the unstoppable approach of eternity—of what he had pondered as a child, but had been unable then to imagine. Again night fell, again he left the Métro in order to begin his long journey across Paris anew—perhaps one of his last, he mused. Yet having taken several steps, he once again felt the iron band squeeze his chest with a more merciless force than he had ever before experienced. He wanted to cry out but could not; then everything slipped away and vanished. He did not notice how they lifted him up, how they placed him in the ambulance, how they drove him to the hospital.

For several days he was delirious, since it turned out that, quite beside everything else, he had pneumonia, accompanied by a high temperature. Strains of the *Boléro* hazily came to him, broken suddenly by powerful trumpet calls whose significance he could not comprehend. The doctor who approached his bed the following morning stopped and listened in amazement: the old beggar, who yesterday had been lifted up off the street, was talking as though he were arguing with an imaginary acquaintance. Yet he was speaking in a very pure and correct English. When he recovered his senses, on the third day, the doctor asked him:

"How is it that you know English?"

Verdier looked at him with his inexpressive, extinguished eyes and replied that he had graduated from university in England.

"In England," said the doctor. "So that's it."

In the dead of night, Verdier, registered as number forty-four, awoke because he thought that somebody's commanding voice was calling him. The patient got up from his bed, stood on the stone floor in his bare feet, took several steps, collapsed and died.

However, in those intervening twenty-four hours that separated the morning of the day when the doctor had asked the patient how it was that he had come by his knowledge of English and the subsequent morning, a colossal administrative machine had been set in motion, and what no one had suspected until now became known. In one of the evening papers an article was printed in which everything was explained: Verdier's nervous attack, which had been accompanied by a loss of memory, and his sudden disappearance. It was suggested that he had spent many years abroad and had returned to France only after the sudden remembrance of everything that had foregone his mental illness.

Thereafter, Verdier's body was claimed by his heirs. A solemn funeral took place, and Verdier was laid to rest in the family crypt. His name was written in gold letters on a duskily glittering slab of dark-grey marble. The consummation of his life was externally exactly as it ought to be, and this was, ultimately, a victory for the world he had renounced a quarter of a century previously. It could be termed a victory for that world—but only if one were to concede that the meaning of the word "victory" outgrows the boundaries of human life, penetrating where there are no boundaries, no life, no meaning, no words.

IVANOV'S LETTERS

(1963)

Whenever I met Nikolai Franzevich, which happened every two or three weeks, I would always have the impression that this man, judging by his nature, by his manner of speaking, by the way he dressed and by his whole demeanour, was a living anachronism, though in the most positive sense of the word. It appeared that he, having been born and raised during the days of the Russian Empire, had remained just as he was back then, and the fact that imperial Russia had long since receded into the past did not in any way tell on him. In terms of his convictions, however, he was no conservative; he avoided speaking of politics, read contemporary authors, attended exhibitions of contemporary painting, listened to music by contemporary composers, though his views on all this were distinguished by a rather emphatic academicism. Of course, there could be nothing more primitive at first sight than some works of so-called abstract painting, but in their own right these searches for a new form in art were an entirely natural thing. The same also applies to contemporary music, which not infrequently sets our teeth on edge. Perhaps we are witnesses to the rebirth of taste, a change of tempo, some, if you will, biological shock whose manifestation sometimes takes on a form that seems controversial to us, or even downright inadmissible. Yet the interchange of styles from a historical perspective is ultimately not only an inevitable phenomenon, but also a rightful one.

Nikolai Franzevich arose in my memory as a character from some unwritten book, as a figment, blatantly the product of someone's imagination, depicted in some detail, but in whom the unknown author had not succeeded in imbuing a real life, which was why this protagonist seemed somewhat artificial, hypothetical and unfinished in the sense that he lacked that day-to-day credibility that any washerwoman or accountant had. I cannot say what explained this impression I was unable to shake, all the more so since there was nothing so farfetched about Nikolai Franzevich. I had the feeling that he never told the whole story, or else was hiding something, although he seemingly had nothing to hide. Never has the word "seemingly" been so used in relation to a person as it was to him. He was seemingly from some province in the north. He had seemingly once lived in the Near East. He was married, seemingly. He had seemingly been a man of great wealth in his day. He seemingly wrote articles on economic matters. He had seemingly completed his education abroad.

Nikolai Franzevich would occasionally invite friends over—three or four people—and would treat them to a very fine repast. His apartment was a rather spacious affair in one of Paris's quieter districts, on the Right Bank of the Seine. On the walls were hung paintings, most often depicting sailing ships at sea and beaches with palm trees, while centre stage was taken by a wonderfully produced copy of a burning frigate by Turner. In one of the corners of the main room towered a twisted column of dark wood; on it, beneath a glass bell, was a clock, which, in place of a pendulum, had something like a flashing brass weathervane swinging back and forth. In Nikolai Franzevich's study there were cabinets filled with books on miscellaneous subjects. One of them was dedicated to travel—Marco Polo, Livingstone, Stanley, Przhevalsky, and the works of several little-known authors who in the Middle Ages reached the wilds of far-flung countries, as well as books on zoology, biology and cultural history. In another cabinet there were French authors—Saint-Simon, Bossuet, La Rochefoucauld, Montaigne, Pascal, Descartes.

His apartment contained some bronze statuettes, among them, for reasons unknown, one of a low-browed man with a general's epaulettes.

The table at Nikolai Franzevich's was waited on by a taciturn woman of middling years, with full lips and dark eyes set against a very pale face, with a distinctive expression of undisturbed sorrow. She forever wore a black dress, and her appearance was as if she had just returned from a funeral. When I once asked Nikolai Franzevich about her, he replied that she was Italian, that Italian women dearly love black and that she wore it because one of her cousins had recently died in Sicily—a cousin whom she had known as a child and had not seen in twenty years. I never once heard her raise her voice; she would reply almost inaudibly, moving her full red lips, which created an impression of contrast with those black dresses, the sorrowful, pale pace and all her funereal aspect.

Just as Nikolai Franzevich altered neither his customs nor his mode of dress, so too the years seemingly (again this "seemingly") passed for him without trace. He remained exactly the same: thick grey hair, deep lines across his forehead, faded eyes. I could never imagine him young. "That's quite understandable," one of our mutual friends once told me, "for he never has been young. Simply one fine day, somewhere in pre-revolutionary Petersburg, a dapper middle-aged man took an apartment and installed himself in it, and this, properly, was the birth of Nikolai Franzevich, whom some celestial power had cast down to our earth perfectly formed, like a parachutist in full kit."

In any case, I had known Nikolai Franzevich for many years and, whereas those people around him grew old and bald, ailed and died, he remained just the same as he had been when I first met him. Granted, he had no destructive passions that could have aided and abetted his premature decline—he did not drink, did not pass sleepless nights at the card table, seemingly did not know the devastating infatuations of the heart—but simply lived well, ate heartily, rose early, took baths, strolled in the Bois de Boulogne, talked with friends and spent the summer in Switzerland or on the Riviera; and in the month of October, when the autumn rains began in Paris, he would return to his apartment and once again that mute, silent woman in mourning garb would look after him, see to it that he had everything he required, right down, perhaps, to those comforts of an emotional nature, the propensity for which her expressive lips and dark eyes betrayed, concealing therein the potential for some other expression, which, incidentally, none of us ever witnessed in her.

Nikolai Franzevich was a fine conversationalist, one of the best I ever chanced to meet. I do not recall his ever arguing with someone, and when I remarked on this to him, he said:

"You see, my friend, I consider arguing a useless business. I converse, let's say, with such-and-such a person. What interests me? What he thinks and how he thinks. My task is that of any interlocutor: to help him express his own thoughts and to familiarize myself with them. I should even say that the less they coincide with my own views, the more interesting it is for me. The intent that is completely alien to me is to try to convince my colleague of the necessity to think as I do. If you lead this to its logical conclusion, you will observe that the achievement of such an aim would lead to the man beginning to repeat your own words, and the conversation would lose any interest. For interest starts where there is difference between people and their opinions."

Nikolai Franzevich did not often lack (despite the fact that he desired to convince no one of anything) for certain didactic motives. He read broadly, books of the most diverse nature, right down to fashionable novels. He would discourse on literature very willingly.

"Human life is impoverished: the vast majority of people cannot truly see what is going on around them, and so-called life experience consists more often than not in a few dozen banal observations. Yet a great many people (that is, so-called readers) tend to have a constant desire for something that they cannot find in their own lives, some other understanding, some other possibilities. They lack the imagination to envisage it without outside help. That, in point of fact, is literature and art's *raison d'être*, though principally literature's. But then, you see, some nations have professional mourners. Their role is to replace those who are unable to express their feelings appropriately, in this instance grief—because a loved one has died. So the mourner, who has never seen the deceased in person and has not the slightest notion of him, for an appropriate compensation weeps over him, as neither his sons nor his wives are able. There is a whole category of writers who perform almost the same function with regard to readers. Such, for example, among Russian writers was Nekrasov. This, however, constitutes only one branch of literature, though a rather significant one."

As far as I recall, Nikolai Franzevich was not a member of a single professional body, though very frequently he would attend meals that were given to mark the anniversary of some activity of some personage. He never gave speeches, but he attentively followed everything that was said, even jotted down some things in his notebook and generally evinced uncommon interest. He was curious to know why Ivan Petrovich had become a barrister while Pyotr Ivanovich had become a doctor, what had determined their callings and when this had come about. He also read the newspapers attentively, took cuttings of them—some unusual incident, a piece about some crime, the memoirs of a famous personality. In his private dealings, Nikolai Franzevich was exceedingly courteous, would say nice things to everyone, speak of everyone with invariable benevolence, and from the sidelines it seemed as if he lived in an idyllic world composed of fine and pleasant people, his many acquaintances.

There was one thing he did not like—people paying him visits without prior warning. Those who did not know this and wanted to call on him without having agreed it in advance would never find him at home, although it often happened that on the day when he was "not at home", and at the hour when somebody arrived at his apartment and no one answered the bell, Nikolai Franzevich was at precisely that time speaking to someone on the telephone and must have been there. At one time a rumour went about that Nikolai Franzevich was not what he seemed; somebody even said that he had dealings with the "intelligence services". Yet this was so far-fetched that even those who repeated it did not themselves believe it. Moreover, there were people who had known Nikolai Franzevich back in Russia, although they were all significantly older than he and approaching that age when the fallibility of memory was as plain as it was forgivable. One of these characters, the former senator Trifonov, a most handsome grey-bearded old chap, with a face cut by deep lines in every conceivable direction—vertical, horizontal, semi-circular—would tell how Nikolai Franzevich carried on in his youth an affair with some celebrated actress, who gave up the stage because of him and ended her life by suicide. Yet former senator Trifonov told this story only once, and when he was later asked to repeat it, he could no longer make the effort of memory necessary. He died soon thereafter, having fallen asleep never again to awake, one winter's night in Paris, during the Thirties of this century, denying us all the chance ever to know whether, besides in his enfeebled memory or frail imagination, there had truly existed somewhere this unknown and celebrated actress who ended her life by suicide because of Nikolai Franzevich.

Nikolai Franzevich, however, continued living in that same apartment, on that quiet street where there was so little traffic that in several spots green grass shot up through the macadam. Under the eaves of the buildings along this street pigeons were forever perching and flying off, there was always silence all around, and only every now and then, from one of the apartments, would the sound of a piano ring out. Yet at nine o'clock in the evening everything would die down, and the footfalls of the odd passer-by could be heard with exceptional clarity. This street in particular seemed to suit Nikolai Franzevich: here one could spend many years without knowing the Elysian Fields, the Grands Boulevards, Montmartre, just as people may live in Tambov, Vologda or Avignon, reading Plutarch or Bossuet before bed and contemplating the vanity of everything in existence, in a state of quiescent meditativeness—the preserve of the few who are happy in their own way.

It seemed beyond doubt that Nikolai Franzevich ranked among them and that everything predisposed him precisely to this. However, what nobody ever knew was the means by which Nikolai Franzevich subsisted. He was employed nowhere and did not work. He did not possess any fortune and, when he had turned up in Paris all those years ago, he had, according to the accounts of those who knew him well then, no money and initially found himself in dire straits, enduring privations with that sense of dignity that never deserted him. On the other hand, he could not have amassed a fortune in Paris, since he had no hand in any business ventures. No inheritance had come his way either—he did not even appear to have any relatives abroad. That he did not engage in illegal dealings and that he was never threatened with prosecution, there could be no doubt.

I once encountered him, late at night, at a dinner organized by the Union of Foreign Journalists in Paris, where I happened to be quite by chance, enticed by the entreaties of one of my acquaintances, a writer for some of the Austrian and Swiss papers, who spent the larger part of his time in innumerable bars and restaurants, so that it was unclear when he could have actually worked. The dinner was not at all bad, though regrettably accompanied by so many speeches given in various languages, the contents of which were always more or less the same: "We live in terrible times, and the responsibility we bear before our readers demands of us… Public opinion cannot remain indifferent… While the threat of tyranny hangs over Europe… We cannot allow…"

A great quantity of wine had been consumed beforehand, after the wine followed cognac, and my acquaintance, with whom I had arrived, managed within a very short period of time to drink the same quantity of wine and cognac that his colleagues drank over the course of the entire evening; he became rowdy and applauded the speakers, and in his befogged imagination there arose a whole set of fantastic visions, blurred and unsteady, such as his colleagues, who soon lost the clarity of their outlines, and a teetering row of black dinner jackets above a white table cloth bespattered with pale-red dots of spilt wine. And over this undulating and moving vision, with a peculiar and drunken cogency, rang out words of responsibility and of the impossibility of allowing—although in actuality there was no responsibility, nor any possibility or impossibility of allowing or not allowing anything; yet for a certain while it seemed not only to my acquaintance, but to his colleagues as well, that the fate of the world hung on what they would write or not write in their articles. It was clear that this strange aberration had been prompted variously by several causes, for which it would be difficult to find any definite explanation: the vintage of the wine and the cognac, which governed subtle changes in its effect, the degree of temporary atrophy in their analytical faculties; however, for those who remained sober, all this seemed a flagrant rejection of elementary and self-evident logic. Luckily, there were few such sober people there, and all that they could have said would have seemed unconvincing to those who spoke of duty and responsibility.

I left this dinner at the same time as Nikolai Franzevich, who, as always, had drunk with gusto, although not to excess. It was a winter's night with that distinctive cold Parisian fog, through which the murky, luminescent blurs of the street lamps spectrally emerged.

He said that he enjoyed taking occasional walks around the deserted nocturnal city. I replied that I shared this partiality of his, and we walked together in the direction of the Seine. Amid the winter fog, which now grew denser in places, now thinned, the incomparable vistas of Paris's streets were unveiled and concealed. In this neurotic light, in this mix of fog and murky blue light from the street lamps, Nikolai Franzevich, in his black overcoat, white silk scarf and bowler hat, seemed to me that night even less convincing than usual. He was of average height, a rather thickset man, and was, on first appearance, just like thousands upon thousands of his peers. And yet I was never able to shake off the impression that a part of him remained unrealized and almost phantom-like. I asked after his health, although over the many years of our acquaintance I could not recall his ever having been ill. He replied that at his age there were always minor ailments, although they had not yet grown to catastrophic proportions… As with all healthy people, this subject clearly bored him. Then he said that what in fact interested him more than anything was how a man lived or what he did.

"Please understand," he said. "I'm convinced that everyone, or nearly everyone, is interested not in how he lives, but in how he wants or ought to live. Many people, as you know, see themselves not as others see them. The vast majority know or suspect they know a few truths. Firstly, that they are not as other people think; secondly, that they live not as they ought to live, by force of a whole host of accidents, because unfavourable circumstances compel them to lead just such an existence. Thirdly, that they deserve a better lot than that which has fallen to them. Finally, and perhaps most importantly: the majority of people feel constrained by those conditions that determine their existence. Their soul, their intellect demand something else, as though each of them needs to live several lives, and not just one."

"But does it not seem to you, Nikolai Franzevich," I said, "that if that really were so, it would be some gross aberration, such as the one that you and I have just attended? In this particular instance, there was talk, was there not, of responsibility, which allegedly rests with those people who today delivered these pathetic tirades on the subject, about which they have, if not an entirely fantastical notion, then a most exaggerated one, to put it mildly?"

"Any notion surpassing very narrow, commonplace boundaries may be an aberration. Even those ideas of a primitive nature—from the viewpoint of a philosophically minded person—such as progress or democracy—truly, are these not aberrations? Yet millions of people have perished because of them. Ultimately it is of no consequence whether it is an aberration or not. It is a sensation, a feeling, a need. And if this were not so, if people did not need to change their lives, there would be none of what we term cultural history."

On this winter's night, the streets of Paris were deserted. From the fog that stretched out before us, the figures of two policemen appeared and disappeared as they made their round, and Nikolai Franzevich said that this for some reason reminded him of *The Night Watch*, although the appearance of these policemen scarcely had anything in common with Rembrandt's famous painting. Next to float out of the fog was the figure of a poor tramp, muffled up in torn overcoat and audibly shuffling his feet in worn-out boots without laces. When this shuffling, like short, dry sobs, had faded away, Nikolai Franzevich said:

"There's yet another victim of aberration for you: that man, who might have been a farmhand somewhere in Auvergne or Normandy, a bricklayer, a dustman, a labourer or a miner, and whose life was also too constrained for him."

Then Nikolai Franzevich said that sometimes—very rarely, mind, on such winter's nights as these—Paris would suddenly begin to remind him of Petersburg.

"Please note that these cities are absolutely dissimilar to one another. But that is immaterial. Here one experiences a feeling that's difficult to define, and it causes an arbitrary impression of similarity that doesn't exist in reality. And that is when you realize that time, years, distance—all these notions are exceedingly relative and deceitful. Time marches on by itself; we live until some mechanical force restores the calendar's truth. But really, time does not exist. We have memories, imagination, we can delve into the past, fear the future, but we term it thus—past, present, future—I think, only because we do not make for ourselves the trouble of contemplating this and understanding that all this is mere sensation."

We were walking along the embankment of the Seine. In the nocturnal fog, the river was invisible, and it began to seem to me more and more that it was the ghost of a man walking beside me—a man who, perhaps, had never really existed, and never more clearly than on that night did Nikolai Franzevich seem so far from the reality in which he and I lived and beyond which I did not know him.

On the deserted Elysian Fields, he and I parted; he got into a taxi and headed homeward. I imagined him returning to his apartment, turning on the light in the room in which, silently and interminably, Turner's blazing frigate burned, then lying down in bed and plunging into the oblivion from which he would again emerge the following morning.

Some time later, when I, along with others, was invited again to supper at Nikolai Franzevich's, he appeared before us as we had always known him—unvaryingly hospitable, exceptionally gracious and a marvellous host. The maid, with her tragic aspect and full red lips upon that pale face, served oysters, Nikolai Franzevich poured white wine, time passed unnoticed, while behind the windows' strained curtains there was a cold winter's evening. Meanwhile, at the table, Petersburg again emerged, about which Nikolai Franzevich spoke willingly and at length: a musical drama, the names of celebrated actors and actresses, Blok's poetry, Hofmann's concerts, the Neva, those inevitable quotations from *The Bronze Horseman*. All this contained a comforting illusoriness, the triumph of memory and imagination—and that evening it seemed to me that Nikolai Franzevich could with the very same ease be transported to another country and another era. For the first time we appreciated him as an extraordinary raconteur—until now he had seemed only a conversationalist. By the time we left, it was already late at night.

Several days later, one of my friends, who had dined with us that evening at Nikolai Franzevich's, said to me:

"I have the most pleasant recollection of that evening. But did you not think there was something queer about it?"

"Queer? No. Though I had no idea that our friend was such a wonderful raconteur."

"Did you not think there was something that didn't quite ring true, something apocryphal about those stories, for all their indisputable skill?"

"No, I think that everything happened just as he said it did."

"I do not doubt it. But do you know what impression I had? That Nikolai Franzevich never did live in Petersburg, that he never has in fact seen the city, but made a diligent study of its history, its way of life, all its place names and festivals, everything—it was as if he were reading us excerpts from a book that he had written about it."

"It was well written, in any case."

"Indubitably. Besides, ultimately he is indeed a Petersburger—it was from Petersburg that the late senator Trifonov knew him. Say what you will, though, I do not believe this man."

He launched into long and garbled explanations that were manifestly unconvincing, yet in a paradoxical way they contained something that was difficult to contradict.

And towards the end of the discussion I began to sense that, truly, one fine day we would again arrive at Nikolai Franzevich's, and he would happen not to be at home, and then it would turn out that in the building where he had lived for so many years there had never been any apartment, any Nikolai Franzevich, and that all this—the burning frigate in his drawing room, his maid, the heavy furniture, his dinners and conversations—all this had been the product of my imagination, one winter's night in Paris, mixing with the fog and the taste of oysters and wine.

All this took place before the war, in those times which later would begin to seem idyllic and be plunged into the depths of the past, like those final years of the Russian Empire. Yet after the war, too, everything continued as it had always done: the same apartment, the same frigate, the same silent maid (on whom time seemingly never told either). Seemingly no course of history could alter anything in Nikolai Franzevich's unconvincing yet indestructible outlook. Despite his advanced age, he maintained exceptional health and a hearty appetite and seemingly never fell ill. However, in all the many years of my acquaintance with Nikolai Franzevich, never once did I see him laugh. His life passed by as though without any difficulties; there were seemingly no tragedies in it, nor could there be. Yet sometimes he would suddenly strike me as a man for whom something distressing prevented his living with that serene ease that should have been his lot—as though amid his cloudless existence something were not as it ought to be, an awareness of guilt, a gnawing regret. Most likely, I thought, neither this guilt nor this regret really existed and were but arbitrary notions, just like that of the imaginary insubstantiality of his positive life.

There then came a time when I had to leave Paris for some considerable while, and I saw Nikolai Franzevich far less often. Thus passed several years, during which his mode of life never altered, as my friends related to me in letters. One day, however, I received a telephone call informing me that Nikolai Franzevich was dead.

The night before I received the news, my friends had dined with him, and, according to their accounts, not one of them could have conceived that they were seeing him for the last time. Everything had been as usual: he received his guests just as courteously, ate with his usual appetite, was just as gracious and kind, and seemed to be in perfect health. The following day he got up at ten o'clock in the morning, the maid drew his bath, he lowered himself into the water, and then she heard a noise like a brief sob—she entered the bathroom and found him dead. Thereafter followed the church, the service, the requiem, and so Nikolai Franzevich was buried in one of Paris's cemeteries, and after a short while a marble slab was placed above his grave, bearing the inscription: "Here lies…"

Thus ended the long life of Nikolai Franzevich, a venerable and respected man who lived in a fine apartment, travelled abroad, read Descartes and Bossuet, was a marvellous conversationalist and host; who, for so many years, knew neither cares nor want, bequeathed to his faithful maid his fine apartment, the wonderful furniture and, as it came to light a little later, a certain sum of money. Thinking on Nikolai Franzevich's death, I recalled a speech that had been given by one of our mutual friends during the funeral service.

"Gentlemen, we are here to bury one of our long-standing friends—he was one of those few people about whom no one can say anything negative and whom no one could ever reproach. He was the living incarnation of all that we consider positive principles in our life. Every man has in his past deeds that he later has cause to regret, instances when he acted not as he ought to have done—such, ultimately, is human nature. Nikolai Franzevich was a happy exception to this rule: never a single negative action, never ill will towards anyone."

Our mutual friend who gave this speech had, in his time, graduated from the Law Faculty of Moscow University. His life abroad, however, had developed in such a way that he never had occasion to practise law; his activities centred principally on the stock market, although his vocation was undoubtedly otherwise, and, as he would admit to us, he frequently envisaged himself in court, winning complex cases, seeking justice for the accused and giving speeches built on sound and irrefutable logic. He was full of these unuttered speeches—and so now, at Nikolai Franzevich's funeral, he spoke as if he were defending the memory of the deceased from some imaginary accusations.

"Nikolai Franzevich was not a public figure, not an artist in any field, not even an author of any number of books or theories. Yet the circle of his interests was exceedingly broad. One could meet him in all the museums of Europe. One could find him reading contemporary authors or the blessed Augustine, and no cultural phenomenon eluded his constant and at once benevolent attention. Among this great quantity of disparate things, Nikolai Franzevich always found his own path, his own particular set of views on life and on how one ought to live—a set of views that I would define as the triumph of positive morals.

"There was something else in him that set him apart from all of us. He stood above personal scores, petty practical interests that often poison our lives. He stood, as it were, apart from those garden-variety miseries, from what we, putting it vulgarly, call the prose of daily existence. He was devoid of ambition; never did he strive to usurp someone's position, to impose his views on someone, and I cannot imagine that Nikolai Franzevich could in any way be indebted to anyone. Conversation with him was always stimulating and fruitful—he belonged to that breed of people who take nothing from others, but willingly share with everyone their exceptional wealth of thoughts and ideas. His personal fate was shaped in such a way that in his life there were, as far as we know, no tragedies, no trials. Yet those to whom they did fall could always count on his understanding and sympathy. He was a man of rare independence, and his sense of self-worth never left him under any circumstance. And if he were to have found himself in a difficult position—which thankfully did not happen during his lifetime—this sense of independence and self-worth would not have left him, and he would have remained just as he does in our memories—a benevolent, cultivated, intelligent, direct and honest man—a sufficiently rare combination of qualities, which in particular bears highlighting when talking of the deceased. He was a Christian—and if you imagine that for him, too, the Day of Judgement will come, he will face this court with a pure soul and a pure heart, and the judges will see that he lived his life without committing a single negative act, without deceiving anyone, without offending, and always trying to understand those who were granted the happiness, as were we all, to be his friend and his grateful contemporaries."

Several days after Nikolai Franzevich's funeral, in the evening, as I was sitting at home, the telephone rang. I lifted the receiver and heard an indistinct woman's voice saying something in very rapid French, but in such agitation and with such a thick accent that at first I was unable to make anything out and decided that my caller must have dialled a wrong number. Then I finally realized: it was Nikolai Franzevich's housekeeper calling to say that she very much wanted to see me. I arranged a meeting for the following morning.

She arrived—in her black mourning dress, just as pale as always—and, fixing her still eyes upon me, explained that she did not know what to do and what was necessary to undertake in order to receive the legacy left to her by Nikolai Franzevich. She showed me his will, which had been attested by a notary. In the will it was succinctly written that everything belonging to Nikolai Franzevich was left to her. I explained to the Italian woman that, as far as I could see, she should have no difficulties and that she should refer herself to the notary. She thanked me and then said:

"He has a lot of papers in a foreign language. I don't understand what's written there and don't know what to do with them. Perhaps you would take a look at them?"

"Very well," I said. "If they are of a private nature, I shan't read them and it will be simplest of all to destroy them."

After this, we made our way to Nikolai Franzevich's apartment—to that quiet street where he had lived for so many years. As before, the trees were wild with verdure, up above was that same deep-blue sky, but now it seemed to me that amid all this calming scenery—two rows of tall buildings, trees, sky—the air was suffused with slow waves of a distant and meditative sadness that had not existed in this street, in this air, while Nikolai Franzevich was still alive. We ascended to the first floor, the Italian woman going before me, and I involuntarily noticed the elastic ease with which her legs overcame the lazy, modest steps of the marble staircase. How old might this woman be? Forty? Forty-five?

The drawers of Nikolai Franzevich's enormous bureau were stuffed with folders of letters, of which there turned out to be many. All the letters were written in English, and they were all addressed to a certain Ivanov who lived on rue Mouffetard—far from the district in which Nikolai Franzevich's apartment was located. A copy of Ivanov's original letter was attached to each of these replies. The letters were addressed to various charitable organizations and to several private individuals, always in faraway countries, chiefly in America, Australia, New Zealand and South Africa. I extracted one of them—several pages in length. In this letter, sent to a private address in California, Ivanov wrote:

Until very recently I had considered my situation hopeless and therefore decided not to bother you with any more requests. Long ago I reconciled myself to my lot and to the cruel fate that ordained that my wife, who might have helped me, be deprived of this ability, for she, after the meningitis that very nearly robbed her of her life, has been left almost totally blind. I picture to myself the cold gloom she is now submerged in, in this wretched flat of ours, where the stove lies long unlit (since we have no money for coal). Sometimes I think I could turn the world upside down if my strength were returned to me. But I am still paralysed—and until only recently felt as if I had been lying in the grave so very long—the difference between my corpse and those buried in cemeteries being that my eyes are open and fate has taken everything from me, except for the capacity to suffer and to watch the suffering of this wretched blind woman, whom I recall as a young girl, laughing, full of strength and hope for the future. In these moments it seems to me that death itself would be a thousand times better, a thousand times easier, a thousand times worthier than the fitful simulacrum of existence I now lead.

Forgive me for writing to you about all this. But you have done so much for me, I am so indebted to you that, separated from you by an enormous distance, I consider you my distant friend—and so I write to you as to a friend. Do you know that this is the first letter I have written to you by myself? I used to dictate my letters, because my hand would not obey my will. Yet several days ago I noted, on a sudden, that I was able to move my right hand. It was a feeling of such tremendous power, it seemed such a miracle, that when I touched this resurrected hand to my face, I found it wet with tears of joy, which I had not until then noticed. The doctor told me that this could just be the beginning, that in future I may yet move the left one, too—and who knows, perhaps after some time I shall stand tall again, as I once did all those many years ago, before I was struck down by paralysis. That is to say, it means I shall again be capable of work—and, whenever I think of this prospect, I find it difficult to breathe from excitement.

Further down there came a detailed description of Ivanov's life, into which from time to time he would insert reflections of a different order.

Sometimes I feel ready to laugh at myself, for I have always held a naive and idyllic dream, a utopian vision of a world in which there is no poverty, no suffering, no envy, a world that is built on a great and complex system of harmonious and happy equilibrium. But I digress. If life be movement, then until very recently I would have been well within my right to consider myself dead.

This long epistle was written with endless digressions and constituted a verbose appeal for financial assistance. Pinned to the copy of this letter was a slip of paper: "Replied 29/11. California, 16/12, cheque No. 437."

Another letter was addressed to Melbourne. Therein Ivanov wrote that he had returned from a sanatorium and was once again at home: a narrow iron bed, the dankness of a small room, the same low ceiling whose curvature sometimes reminded him of the vault of a crypt.

Further down:

I am forced to spend a lot of time in bed, since I have no strength for anything else. During these long hours I think about many things. My first thought is to turn to God and to be grateful that I am alone and that this slow death, which has pervaded the very atmosphere in which I have lived all these long years, will harm no one. In the end, what does it matter if the world does not hear the symphonies that are engendered in my imagination and the sounds that attend me everywhere? After my death, people will say that here died a man who thought himself a composer, though he wrote nothing. Who in the end will know that this whole ocean of sounds that engulfs me came into being precisely at the moment when this unrelenting illness deprived me of the ability to set down these symphonies and to harness this impetuous motion of sounds, beyond which I cannot conceive of life?

In this instance, Ivanov was a composer, who was slowly dying of consumption and who had been advised by doctors that improved nutrition and a trip to the Maritime Alps could save him. But for this he needed means. The composer asked himself the question: did he have the moral right to appeal to a complete stranger for help? He believed he could write such things, which no one before him had written. But perhaps this was just an illusion, perhaps he had no musical gift? So came meditations on the nature of artistic creation.

Perhaps Beethoven's symphonies existed before he was born. And that distinction which we call genius—and which we cannot call otherwise—consists in his having been the only person in the world to hear these sounds, that is, the music that, but for him, no one heard. So the question, then, is this: did he create these eternal symphonies, did he create this unique world of sounds—or did he just hear and set down for all what had always been there? If the latter, then perhaps I, too, can hear the sounds that, by dint of millions upon millions of accidents, no one apart from me knows.

I sat with Ivanov's archive for several hours. I could but be amazed by the assortment of quotidian details he included in his letters. In some cases he was a lonely man. Others made reference to a wife who had been taken seriously ill. Irrespective, however, of any mention of family or otherwise, Ivanov himself was always at death's door.

I know that I am gradually going blind and that nothing can prevent this. When my eyes no longer see, I shall take away with me the visual memory of the world that now is slowly dimming and becoming obscured from my intense gaze. No longer shall I see, but I shall never forget these contours that I have seen for so many years, this dynamism of lines, this play of coloured reflections on the water, these elusive transitions from azure to navy, from turquoise to azure, which I traced from the deck of a ship at sea. I know that for the remainder of the time allotted to me I shall hear innumerable sounds in the dark, but in this world I shall feel alien, and I hardly imagine that I shall grow accustomed to this blinded universe: without light, without sun, without dusk—without night?

In another letter Ivanov—who had recently (or so he said) been run over by a motor car—wrote:

What I feel more than anything is a pain in the toes of my right foot—a feeling that proves to me a single truth that I had never before suspected. We believe—and I always believed so—that imagination is the result of mental activity. By "imagination" I mean the notion of what in reality does not exist, and what you English call fiction, a word that is difficult to translate into other languages. Now I am convinced that this is not so. Our muscular and nervous system—this seemingly inanimate assemblage of tissue and nodes—is also possessed of imagination. For what other than the imagination in muscles and nerves could explain this feeling in the toes of an amputated leg?

Another thought: what a curious profession—the maker of artificial arms and legs, and what a singular branch of industry!

The contents of this letter, which was just as long as the others, led up to Ivanov's needing to buy an artificial leg and his lack of money for the purchase. Indeed, all his letters contained an appeal for help—but sometimes this appeal was not expressed directly. Each letter was a tale, and they were all written in such a tone, as though Ivanov were addressing people who could not fail to understand him, who along with him were inclined to contemplate the vicissitudes of fate and the woeful lot of their correspondent. In almost every letter Ivanov asked himself the question: did he in fact have the moral right to ask anyone for help? This question, however, was of a purely rhetorical nature.

Among those to whom Ivanov sent these letters were, by all accounts, the most diverse people, which was evident from their content. One could but wonder at the range of topics Ivanov discussed—topics that always depended upon the addressee of the letter. He would write on the economic development of the world, on the transformation of various forms of capitalism, on politics, on the destiny of France and its historical past, on Western culture. There were letters that dealt with the last ages of Byzantium, painting, literature—in all this Ivanov displayed exceptional erudition. However, a particularly pathetic tone was reserved for those letters dispatched to people of a spiritual calling and making reference to religion. With that same unfaltering inspiration Ivanov wrote on Catholicism ("ultimately, the history of Christianity is the history of the Catholic Church, regardless of what people may say, whatever the horrors of the Inquisition, which dissolve and vanish in the true and eternal Rebirth of Christian faith in the incomparable radiance of Our Saviour"), on Lutheranism ("only Luther, only he, grasped the danger of Christianity's ossification, of the petrification and rigidity of its iconography—without him we should not know the meaning of true faith"), on Buddhism ("if we are to assert objectively that the fundamental distinction between monotheistic religion and various types of pagan faiths—examples of which are given us from Hellas and Rome, among others—consists in the fact that meditation and spiritual contemplation are extraneous to paganism and without them we cannot imagine monotheism, then a religion in which the main role is played by this solemn act of contemplation is naturally Buddhism"). To each letter was affixed a small slip of paper with the dates of its dispatch, reply and cheque.

I pored over these letters for several hours. In each of them Ivanov transformed: after an architect appeared an engineer, after the engineer a former history teacher. As I read them, I pondered what agonizing labours of imagination were required of the author of these letters. After all this, there could no longer be any doubt, of course, about the source of Nikolai Franzevich's income: the second apartment in a poor district of Paris, the falsified documents in the name of some Ivanov who had never existed, and the persistent toil of many years. Several times the Italian woman came into the study where I was sitting and then left. I eventually told her, sans explanation, that she could destroy these letters. Then I bid her farewell and went home.

It was a summer's evening. I was sitting in my armchair and thinking about what I had just learnt. The fact that, in the end, there had never been any Ivanov did not seem so important to me. Of minor importance, too, was the fact that this was how Nikolai Franzevich had made his money. What truly mattered was that Nikolai Franzevich, the man we knew and remembered, did not exist either, despite his deceptive corporeality—the apartment, the dinners and the Italian woman. The fluidity of form in which his existence had passed, that improbable array of metamorphoses to which his letters attested, all these were, perhaps, his spasmodic and unsuccessful attempts at incarnation, the fruitless striving to find his place in the world, which, for reasons unknown, had long been lost, like a recollection of the past that no effort of memory or imagination is capable of resurrecting. And what was more, no meditative philosophy or edifying reading of Bossuet or Descartes could have saved Nikolai Franzevich—insofar as he existed—from the constant lying, from the consciousness of his gnawing guilt before these guileless people to whom he wrote his letters and to whom he turned in the name of those positive principles— of which his life was a cruel and irredeemable negation. It was all was myth and chimera—his philosophy, his life, Ivanov's epistolary literature—it was all untrue and deceitful, right down to the calendar date of his funeral, for Nikolai Franzevich, whom I had known for so many years and in whose reality I could never fully bring myself to believe, disappeared and vanished within that empty grave, into which his empty coffin had been lowered, not when a speech was made about the non-existent merits of this non-existent person, but several days later, on that summer's evening when I returned home after reading Ivanov's letters.

Pushkin Press

Pushkin Press was founded in 1997, and publishes novels, essays, memoirs, children's books—everything from timeless classics to the urgent and contemporary.

This book is part of the Pushkin Collection of paperbacks, designed to be as satisfying as possible to hold and to enjoy. It is typeset in Monotype Baskerville, based on the transitional English serif typeface designed in the mid-eighteenth century by John Baskerville. It was litho-printed on Munken Premium White Paper and notch-bound by the independently owned printer TJ International in Padstow, Cornwall. The cover, with French flaps, was printed on Rives Linear Bright White paper. The paper and cover board are both acid-free and Forest Stewardship Council (FSC) certified.

Pushkin Press publishes the best writing from around the world—great stories, beautifully produced, to be read and read again.

STEFAN ZWEIG · EDGAR ALLAN POE · ISAAC BABEL
TOMÁS GONZÁLEZ · ULRICH PLENZDORF · JOSEPH KESSEL
VELIBOR ČOLIĆ · LOUISE DE VILMORIN · MARCEL AYMÉ
ALEXANDER PUSHKIN · MAXIM BILLER · JULIEN GRACQ
BROTHERS GRIMM · HUGO VON HOFMANNSTHAL
GEORGE SAND · PHILIPPE BEAUSSANT · IVÁN REPILA
E.T.A. HOFFMANN · ALEXANDER LERNET-HOLENIA
YASUSHI INOUE · HENRY JAMES · FRIEDRICH TORBERG
ARTHUR SCHNITZLER · ANTOINE DE SAINT-EXUPÉRY
MACHI TAWARA · GAITO GAZDANOV · HERMANN HESSE
LOUIS COUPERUS · JAN JACOB SLAUERHOFF
PAUL MORAND · MARK TWAIN · PAUL FOURNEL
ANTAL SZERB · JONA OBERSKI · MEDARDO FRAILE
HÉCTOR ABAD · PETER HANDKE · ERNST WEISS
PENELOPE DELTA · RAYMOND RADIGUET · PETR KRÁL
ITALO SVEVO · RÉGIS DEBRAY · BRUNO SCHULZ · TEFFI
EGON HOSTOVSKÝ · JOHANNES URZIDIL · JÓZEF WITTLIN